undeniable

LOVE

MIA LONDON

Debbie —
from the best!
Mia London

Undeniable Love
by Mia London

Copyright ©2018 Mia London

ISBN - **978-0-9832474-3-2** (ebook)
IBSN - **978-0-9832474-4-9** (pbook)

Publisher: Mia London
PO Box 93852
Southlake, TX 76092

Cover design by Just Write Creations.

Dedication

This book is dedicated to my reader fans. This is my seventh book, Lucky #7. And I feel tremendously lucky to have you. Special thanks to Pam Dunn for giving me encouragement, even if she didn't realize it.

Chapter 1

"I CAN'T FREAKING believe you're moving to Dallas, Texas," Courtney said as she handed her friend a stack of shirts. "It's like you're living a fantasy, a dream, Lil."

Lily Bennett chuckled. "I wouldn't go that far. But it's definitely exciting."

Lily's life had done a one-eighty. She'd met the man of her dreams while on a business trip in Rome—dreams she'd never considered could come true. When she'd returned home from those four magical days, her employer had handed her a pink slip. Not that she held animosity about that; some job loss happened when there was a buyout.

But seriously, how does one wrap up a life, and move halfway across the country? There was so much to do, her mind was spinning.

Holding up a pink bustier, Courtney asked, "Will you have room for this?"

Her cheeks heated and she grabbed the garment from her friend. "Ha. Ha. Very funny. Yes, I'll have room. My new place is about five-hundred square feet bigger. I'm so excited."

"Maybe you should just move in with your billionaire boyfriend."

Lily's head shot up. "No, Court. No way am I moving that fast. We met in—what?—June. And it's only early September. I'm not doing that."

Although those exact thoughts flooded her mind. Brandon had more than hinted at it. On many levels, she was taking a huge leap, especially a leap of faith. She had no idea how to work for the same man she was dating.

"Well, that's fine, but what if he proposes?"

Lily's stomach flipped over multiple times. She dared not let herself think that far ahead.

"One day at a time, Court." She emptied the last drawer from the bathroom vanity and placed the box on the bed to tape.

"I still cannot believe he's the CEO for the same company you interviewed with."

"Right?" Cosmic was the only way Lily could describe it.

"When can I come visit you?"

"Give me some time to get acclimated, and I'll let you know my travel schedule. I never thought I'd be heading back to Rome." Her voice climbed an octave.

Courtney grinned at her. "I should get one of those credit cards that gives miles, and maybe I can go with you."

"Ohmigod, Court! That would be awesome."

"Maybe I'll meet my own handsome billionaire."

The chuckles from the girls grew into laughter, a belly laugh Lily hadn't felt in a while.

Maybe Courtney would meet the man of her dreams in Rome. Court was very much a serial dater—she believed you had to kiss a lot of frogs before you met your prince.

Lily smiled for the rest of the day as they boxed her possessions from her tiny apartment, ready for the movers to arrive the next morning to load boxes and her few pieces of furniture. Funny that after almost twenty years this was all she had. She'd just as soon put her money into travel, than clothes or expensive art.

"I'm gonna miss you."

"I'll miss you too, Lil. You're like a sister to me; we won't lose touch."

"We won't," Lily promised as her eyes clouded.

"C'mon. Let's order pizza."

That night, Lily's head hit the pillow and she instantly fell asleep from sheer exhaustion. A new adventure would begin the next day. She only prayed it was a smart move. Not one she'd live to regret.

Chapter 2

LILY ARRIVED AFTER being away for several days. Brandon greeted her outside DFW airport. Standing beside a limo, he wore a charcoal suit, his pink tie loosened, looking sexy as sin. She'd missed him while she was gone, and seeing him now made her heart full again.

"Hello, handsome."

"Hello, gorgeous." He snaked an arm around her waist and pulled her close. With his free hand, he cupped the nape of her neck and crashed his mouth over hers. She dropped her carry-on on the sidewalk and immediately looped her arms around his neck. His tongue dove into her mouth.

Her knees weakened. Would he always make her feel like this?

After a few beats, he smiled and opened the limo door for her. Inside was a tray of hors d'oeuvres and a bottle of champagne in an ice bucket. She felt like a princess going to the ball.

He said something to the driver and then slid in next to her—the privacy screen already raised so the driver couldn't see them in the back of the luxury car.

"Welcome home, Lily," he said as he opened the bottle of champagne.

"Thank you. And thanks for taking care of moving all my stuff, including my car." She leaned in and placed a quick peck on his lips. Looking down at the tray of food, she said, "This is an incredibly nice greeting," and reached for a piece of jumbo shrimp. Succulent.

He handed her a glass and raised his. "To new beginnings."

She smiled, touching his flute in a toast. "To new beginnings."

They ate, drank, and he filled her in on some company business. In the rush-hour traffic, the car moved slowly. Not that she cared how long it took to get to Brandon's condo. Talking with Brandon over food felt natural, just like in Rome. How she loved hearing him tell stories about work, or his family, or . . . really anything.

"God, I've missed you," he said, breaking the stream of conversation.

Her stomach did another freaky flip. "I don't even think I was gone five days," she replied with a smile. "What are you going to do when I go to Rome for two weeks?"

Without missing a beat, he replied, "Sell the company and fly out there to be with you."

She laughed out loud, and he grinned.

His smile faded as he took the crystal flute from her hand and placed it in a holder next to his.

5

"Come here," he commanded as he straightened in his seat.

She unlatched her seatbelt and hoisted her body over his lap, shimmying her skirt up to straddle him. His hands instantly cupped her face to bring her mouth to his. His tongue slipped passed her lips and danced with hers. The mere touch of his lips sent pleasure coursing throughout her body. He had her body trained to respond to his.

He grabbed her ass and pulled her closer. She moaned at the pressure of his cock against her center.

His hands moved up to her blouse buttons and one-by-one unhooked them. Even though they were out in public, she wanted Brandon inside her. No one could see through the darkened windows. She gasped. *My boss.*

She grabbed at the lapels of her top and yanked them closed. Someone in Brandon's position surely wouldn't risk exposure over something that could wait.

His brow furrowed. "What's wrong?"

"Brandon, I don't know . . . I'm your employee now. We're in a limo . . ."

His face softened. "It's alright. First, no one can see us. Next, we will certainly be more careful at the office."

She shook her head. "I don't want people thinking I got this job because I slept with you . . . sleep with you," she implored. Her face warmed with the embarrassing thoughts.

He kissed her palms. "Don't worry about that," he spoke softly. "Miss Bennett, perhaps we can discuss this later. I would really like to fuck you senseless before we make it back to my place where I do it all again."

Oh God, she would love that. Her heart flip-flopped. Brandon did things to her with his kiss, with his touch, and with his words. She couldn't deny him anything.

He returned to his task and pushed the fabric off her shoulders, when his phone rang.

He let out an expletive and glanced at the screen. Randy somebody. It might have been his VP of Manufacturing, but she wasn't certain.

"It can wait." He silenced the phone and threw it on the seat.

She quickly returned to the moment when he noticed her red bra trimmed in black lace.

He traced a finger over the trim. "This is very nice." His voice held a smooth-like-chocolate richness Lily loved.

"I bought it in Rome."

His eyebrows rose. "Really?"

The question didn't need an answer and Brandon didn't wait. He dragged the straps off her shoulders, exposing her heavy breasts. He pushed on her back, forcing a nipple to his face which he hungrily sucked into his mouth.

"Unh," escaped her lips. The driver might not be able to see, but could he hear them?

Brandon sucked, lapped, and gently bit at her nipples working her into a frenzy. Her hips moved on their own, seeking friction against his hard cock, eager for him to be inside her.

He tunneled his hand between them and easily found her heat. His fingers slid underneath her lace thong and stroked through her wet slit to her clit.

She moaned unabashedly.

"Are you ready, Miss Bennett? You feel ready. Can you handle me? All of me?" She heard the words but as he pushed two fingers inside, her head spun. The more he pumped, the more the blood behind her ears roared.

"Lean back, hands on my knees. I want to see this beautiful pussy mess up my pants as you come all over me."

She did as he bid and rested her forearms on his muscular thighs. He bunched her skirt further up her belly. With her D-cup breasts hanging out of her bra, her skirt pushed up high, and her thong stretched to expose her pussy, she likely looked perfectly debased for him.

He pushed further inside, his knuckles slammed her sex.

"Ah!" she cried out. "Oh, God. Brandon."

His fingers twisted and stroked, and he rammed her again. "Maybe you should call me Mr. Morgan, Miss Bennett."

She heard the amusement in his voice. She breathed out, "Yes, sir."

And before she questioned if she could take anymore, he added a third finger, twisting and stroking her core, sending the orgasm exploding throughout her shaking body.

He gave her a few seconds to recover, helped her upright, and kissed her sweetly, reverently.

Softly, he commanded, "On all fours on the floor, baby."

Oh, could she handle more? She wanted more, despairingly so.

She lifted off his lap, turned facing the front, and went down on the floor of the limo. She glanced over her shoulder to watch Brandon pull his cock in front of a condom to roll it on.

He met her eyes, and never left as he drew her thong over her hips to her knees.

He inhaled deeply. "Lily, you look beautiful like this." With one hand on her hip, and one aligning his cock, he gently pushed inside. They both moaned.

"God, Brandon. You feel bigger."

He leaned forward, his arms bracketing her. "It's because I missed you. I've gone months without you. Now that you've agreed to give us a try, I can't get enough of you."

She moaned again. His words touched her heart. She couldn't remember the last time her heart felt so full, and from a man who only wanted to make her happy. To please her. To be with her. No expectations of what she could do for his status.

His speed increased. "Lil, I don't think I can wait much longer."

Her cheeks burned with heat. Damn if he wouldn't make her come again. If there was time.

He slowed his pace, and exhaled. He caressed her ass in large circles. Then his hands took position and gently pulled her cheeks apart.

She should feel mortified, but her inner muscles fluttered with the gentle beginnings of an orgasm.

"You should see this, baby. You taking me in. Your swollen little lips caressing me like you were made for me, and I for you."

Oh, his words. His cock stroked, pulling back, pushing all the way forward. His hands tugged more, almost to the point of pain, spreading her.

"Oh God." Flutters turned into full-blown muscular contractions. The cataclysmic sensation rocked her core once again. And as she screamed out his name, Brandon growled in her ear, his cock flexing in her pussy.

They both collapsed to the floor. His arms wrapped around her, and tugged her close, spooning his front with her back. He still inside her.

"Wow," she breathed.

His breath slowed as he said softly in her ear. "I'm sorry."

She froze.

"I should have waited until we were home." She heard the regret in his voice.

She eased the detachment and turned toward him. "Don't be. That was amazing. I may not be able to face your driver, but that was amazing and wonderful, and exhilarating."

His lips curved slightly.

"I love what we do," she continued. "And how you make me feel. And the way this all started, I guess I shouldn't expect *ordinary* from you."

He smirked and wove his fingers through her hair. "You make me crazy, in a good way. It's like I'm more alive when I'm with you."

Oh Lord above. Had anyone ever said something so sweet to her like that before?

He pecked the tip of her nose. "We'll be there soon. Let's get dressed." He maneuvered to the bench seat and offered her his hand.

They redressed, trying to look somewhat respectable. What a way to start the next chapter of her life.

Chapter 3

BRANDON SCOLDED HIMSELF a thousand times for taking Lily in the limo. She's not that kind of a woman, he'd repeated.

And when she looked at him with those gorgeous blue eyes, saying she didn't mind, he believed her. She let him do those things to her; she was so damn trusting.

Looking back at all his sexual encounters, he could not recall one time when he'd taken a risk or done something crazy. Only with Lily. Now, it was almost their norm. He could not keep his hands off her.

And fuck, he loved it, and he hoped she'd never stop loving it too.

When they arrived at his condo, she thanked Gerry, briefly making eye contact.

"Sir. Ma'am." Gerry nodded.

She had nothing to worry about. Gerry had been with Brandon since the beginning—back in Miami. He may look old enough to be his father, but he was smart, tactful, and amazingly discreet. Brandon owed the man gratitude for transferring with him to Dallas.

Brandon had a hard time adjusting to Gerry calling him *sir* when he was a mere twenty-four years old, but Gerry had insisted. *Sir, it is for the benefit of those around you. You are in a position of authority.* Brandon accepted that.

He opened the door to his condo, and instantly her eyes lit up at the bouquet of red roses on the coffee table. He loved seeing her like this, so happy. And he couldn't wait to shower her with more gifts.

Not too much too soon, his inner voice warned. She'd told him she didn't want to rush things. He'd try his damnedest to remember that.

"Oh, Brandon, they're beautiful." She kicked off her shoes, dropped her purse on the chair, and rushed to smell her flowers.

Gerry discreetly left the bags by the door and closed it behind him. Alone again.

Brandon inhaled through his nostrils. He needed a distraction or he'd haul her to his bedroom. She deserved a proper greeting.

"How about some wine?"

"Sounds good."

He claimed an open bottle of red from his wine cabinet, and poured them each a glass. She met him in the kitchen.

Handing her a glass, he asked, "So when is the moving truck expected?"

"Mmm, delicious." She took another sip and replied. "Day after tomorrow."

He remained silent, literally biting on his tongue.

"Don't say it," she said, her tone a playful scold.

He set his wine glass on the counter. "I won't say that you should just move in here." He shook his head. "Nope. Although there is more than sufficient room."

"The place is huge," her eyes rounded, emphasizing the last word, "but that's not the point. We haven't spent enough time together to make such a big leap. We need to date. Get to know each other. *Capisce*?"

He sighed. "Yes. So, Miss Bennett, would you go out with me tomorrow night? I'd like to take you on a date."

She grinned from ear to ear, and snuggled closer into him. "I'd love to." Then she pushed on her tiptoes to kiss him.

Before he could take it further, she backed away. "This might be a good time to talk about work." She drank from her glass while keeping eye contact with him.

"Okay. What about work? You want to discuss ground rules?"

"Yes, I think that would be wise. As I said, I don't want people getting the wrong idea."

"Fair enough. What did you have in mind?"

"Well, how do you address everyone? First name or last name?"

"First name."

"Okay, but I hear them address you as Mr. Morgan." Her head tipped some, looking adorable as she tried to play out the scenario in her head.

"Most people do. The only exception is upper management and the board."

"Alright. I will be calling you Mr. Morgan when we are at work."

He nodded. "What's next?"

"No preferential treatment. Treat me just as you would any of your employees."

"Okay."

"No excess time together. We use discretion when calling, texting, or even lunching together."

As much as he wanted to balk, he would be lying. He loved having Lily here in Dallas. Having her working for him. *Wanted* her to move in with him. But he was simply too busy to even break-away most days for lunch. Unless he had a meeting at a restaurant, he'd grab what he could from the executive lunchroom.

"Alright."

"And I don't think there should be any hanky-panky going on either."

"What?" Was she serious?!

"In the office. I mean, in the office." She quickly clarified, and the precious blush crept over her cheeks that made him smile, with relief.

He stepped closer. "I'm so relieved to hear you say that, Miss Bennett." He leaned down to kiss her, starting slowly, but as was often the case, he couldn't stop himself from wanting more.

Her arms looped around his neck causing her plump breasts to press against his chest. His dick quickly got ready for another round.

Shit!

He broke their contact, creating a few inches between them. "Lily, I'm sorry. I need to call Randy back tonight. It shouldn't be long." He spun around to pull a covered dish from the refrigerator. Lifting the aluminum foil, he saw the cook had left some kind of cheesy chicken entree. "I'll put this in the oven, and when it's warm, I should be done with my phone call." Brandon turned on the oven as he spoke.

To her credit, she replied congenially. "No problem. I'll unpack a few things from my luggage."

He grinned. "Unpack as much as you want. You'll find space in the closet." He placed a quick kiss on her lips, and headed to his office.

True to his word, he'd cleared some hanging space and a few drawers for her to leave things. She snickered. He'd *planned* for her arrival and the thought sent flutters to Lily's stomach. *This must be what love feels like.*

She wanted to caution herself against those feelings, but it was too damn late. And he may not feel the same way. Lily was content that he slowly revealed more of himself to her, and that thrilled her to the core.

She didn't mind that he had to work. He had a company to run. People were counting on him. She heaved several suits and dresses to the bar in his enormous closet and closed the door over them. She'd only seen pictures of tricked-out closets like this, where each section had glass doors. Dust-proofing everything, she suspected. Seeing it in person brought it to a whole other level.

Lily grinned and went back to her suitcase for her toiletries. Her first day of work was the following day. She wanted everything just so.

Next she retrieved her smartphone and traded a few texts with Courtney. Several emails came in so she took her time reading and reviewing those. Some junk stuff, a few from human resources that she'd been expecting, and one from her parents who were on a trip in Arizona. She replied to her parents telling them she'd arrived safely and couldn't wait to start her new job. She invited them to Dallas anytime, but her apartment only had one bedroom, so they'd have to get a hotel room.

The oven timer sounded. Lily jumped off the bed and hustled to the kitchen. The room smelled yummy and her stomach growled.

She flipped off the timer and the power to the oven. She searched for oven mitts to lift out the glass dish and set it on top of his six-burner stove.

"You look good in my home."

She spun around and smiled at her handsome temporary roommate. "Dinner's ready."

"Great." He stepped closer and reached in the cabinet for two dinner plates and white wine glasses. She searched for silverware and cloth napkins, and transferred them to the table. He uncorked an expensive-looking bottle of wine. She set the dish on a hot pad in the center of his table. Working side-by-side with him felt effortless and easy.

They sat, and after a brief silence, he spoke softly. "Sitting here with you reminds of the few dinners we had together in Italy."

She smiled and nodded.

They ate a few bites in between conversation.

"So are you ready for tomorrow?"

"I am. I'm excited but nervous too," she told him honestly.

"Nervous? Why?"

"You have a big company, Brandon. There's a lot to learn. Plus the whole Corticelli transition."

Corticelli Labs was the company Brandon had purchased during his trip to Rome. The trip where they'd met and her life changed so dramatically. For the better.

He covered her hand, pulling her focus off her plate to him. "You will be great. Don't put too much pressure on yourself. Training will bring you up to speed on the company, and the transition team will be there to help with Corticelli."

He was probably right. She need not be so hard on herself.

They continued to talk about less stressful things like her family and his. Evidently, Katie, one of his sisters, had been busy planning her wedding. Katie was the sister who had moved out to Dallas, while the other one, Leena, stayed in Miami to run several offices. Katie and Brandon carried the load in Dallas. It sounded like the siblings had a good formula for working together.

"So when does she get married?"

"Um, December second. Then they will take off for a few weeks to Hawaii for a honeymoon. Back in time for Christmas."

He wiped his mouth and pushed his plate away. "Lily, do you have plans for December second?"

She grinned. "I don't think so."

"Would you like to be my date for my sister's wedding?"

"I'd love to."

He pitched forward and placed a slow, easy kiss on her lips, then sat back. "You've had a long day. How about I clean this up and you go take a bath?"

Her eyebrows lifted. *Wow!*

"I bought some bath gel you might like."

She smiled back at him. "That sounds great. My neck muscles feel tight."

He kissed her on the forehead and carried dishes to the kitchen.

A bath sounded like an amazing idea, and Brandon's bathtub was like a mini-swimming pool. She fetched her robe. Turning on the faucet, she stripped and climbed in, forcing the water level to rise over her breasts. Lily took several deep breaths of the lavender oil, which was very soothing and relaxing. She could get used to this.

A light rap came from the doorway. "May I join you?" Her sexy guy leaned against the bathroom door jamb, holding their wineglasses, looking every bit the confident, wealthy businessman who also had an incredible talent for making her feel like a sexy pin-up that men would kill to be with. Well, she didn't care about *men*. She only cared about him, and what he thought of her.

"Yes. Please."

He handed her a glass, half-full, and took a sip of his own before setting it on the vanity.

Brandon proceeded to pull at this tie and shirttails. He unfastened the button from his shirt, then his pants. One piece at a time, his clothing fell to the floor in a pile. Naked before her, he made no attempt to hide his erection.

The beautiful sight of his hard, honed flesh . . .

Inspiration hit her. She turned ninety-degrees to face him and got on her knees. She rested the wineglass on the floor, and asked, "Mr. Morgan, could I see you for a moment?"

He grinned and his amazing eyes darkened.

"Certainly Miss Bennett." Coming to within inches of her face, he continued, "What can I do for you?"

With her right hand she gently wrapped her fingers around his impressive cock. Glancing up, she said, "Sir, it seems that," she leaned forward and

18

licked his swollen head, "some people are complaining about low morale."

He groaned when she returned to her task and closed her lips around him. His hand wove through her hair. "Low morale?"

"Yes sir."

"What do you . . . suggest . . . we do?"

She took more of him into her mouth hitting the back of her throat and sucking on the way up.

Her hand tugged and stroked while she spoke. "I think if more extracurricular activities were available, that would help."

He panted now. "Activities?"

"Mmm," she murmured over his cock. "I'm very fond of cock-sucking, personally."

He groaned. "God, Lily. That mouth."

She sucked more and moved faster. He was close, and she knew it. Brandon slammed his hand on the wall next to him for support. His climax came fast—she pulled back and aimed his cum for the top of her breasts.

He panted and stared down with glassy eyes as she took her hands and rubbed his cum all over her chest, and massaged her breasts for several long moments.

"Fuck, Lily." He bent forward, lifted her to a standing position and wrapped his arms around her, kissing her passionately. "You are the sexiest woman I have ever laid my eyes on."

She kissed him back with as much as he gave. Kissing Brandon was like nothing else. So much of what she did with Brandon couldn't compare to anything in her life. She was on a full-time high.

He gently released her and climbed into the tub behind her. She was wet between the thighs, she knew. Her sex ached. But she'd happily wait for him to recharge, because this was just the beginning.

She rested in front of him, her back to his front.

"You mentioned something about tight shoulders."

She glanced back. "Yes. I think I overdid it these last few days."

He brought his hands out of the water, slid them up her back to her shoulders, and began a slow, deep massage. Oh crap! She should have known Brandon would be good at that too.

She pulled her hair to the side. "You are very good at giving massages."

"Thank you."

"Do you give them a lot?"

She felt him shrug. "Not really."

She moaned when he worked out a particularly stubborn knot. "Do you get them a lot?"

"I've never had a professional massage in my life."

She pivoted toward him, staring in disbelief. "Why not?"

He shrugged again. "No time really. If I need to handle stress, I go to the gym to work it off."

"Wow."

"Now Miss Bennett, I'd like to return to the discussion about your concerns of low morale in the workplace." He lifted a soaked sponge and began to wash her chest, arms, and stomach. "On your knees, please."

She rose, and he scooted forward, taking a nipple into his mouth, kissing and nibbling on each nipple, making her moan.

The sponge made circles over her ass and back, then down her thighs, inside and out. After dropping the sponge, he glossed a finger over her short curls through her wet slit. "What if there was a way I could promise regular orgasms? Do you think that would improve morale?"

His finger dipped inside. "Oh, God."

He added another finger. "I'm waiting."

"Yes, sir. I think that's a brilliant idea."

"Perfect." And with that he pulled his fingers out.

The loss was surprising, but she waited patiently.

He rose and took her hand, tugging her with him. "Come with me, please."

He gingerly wrapped a towel around her and took one himself. He led her to the bedroom, and flipped on the overhead light. Gees! It was bright considering she's strategically *not* turned on all the lights in the bathroom. She hated bright lights especially when she was naked.

He slowly, methodically towel-dried her.

"Now, Miss Bennett, if you'd lie down on the bed, I would like to personally address *your* morale."

She swallowed hard and hesitated. He wasn't turning off the light.

"Miss Bennett?"

"Um, could we turn off the light?"

He stepped closer, completely at ease with his own nudity, and cupped her arms, stroking up and down. "Lily, I love your body, you know this. You know I would grant you anything. Tomorrow, no lights, but tonight, I need to see you. All of you. I need to savor every inch of your skin, see every freckle, every dimple, and every fold of your pussy. I want to taste you from head to toe. You are a feast for my eyes, not just my tongue."

Oh holy crap!

21

What could she say? His words melted her. She silently nodded and dropped her towel, making her way to the center of the bed.

Brandon dug in his nightstand drawer for a condom and quickly sheathed himself. She lay straight as a stick, arms over her stomach. He grinned and stretched out next to her, facing her on his side. He leaned down, capturing her lips with his, his hand resting over hers. His tongue danced with hers, and her hand lifted to grasp the nape of his neck. With her eyes closed, she could imagine they were in the dark.

Brandon's firm, but soft lips moved away from hers, traveling leisurely to her neck. He stroked her hair to the side to gain more access to her throat.

His body warmed hers and his kisses started to ignite the fire that moments ago had burned out.

He shifted his weight over her, and his hands cupped her breasts as he kissed his way down to meet them. He sucked a nipple into his mouth, this time taking more breast with him.

She cried out and arched her back off the bed.

He repeated the treatment to the other breast. Her legs tightened, her thighs mushing together to try and stave off the ridiculous ache he produced.

His kisses traveled down to her stomach and his tongue dipped into her navel. As he continued to kiss, he slowly pushed her legs apart. He licked and kissed down one leg, separating them more, then he kissed and licked her other leg, neglecting her center.

She needed relief. Desperately.

He lifted his mouth and gingerly slid a finger, just barely touching, over her wet slit.

"Look how beautiful." He motioned his finger up her center again, driving her insane with his light touch. "Look how wet you are. It's coming out onto your lips." His finger stroked where he saw her wetness.

Her face felt on fire with the heat, the lust he brought out of her. Brandon did this. Always, making her want more, do more, and all to pleasure her. He always wanted to pleasure her.

He looked directly into her eyes. "You are gorgeous, lying on my bed, spread out for me." He pushed her legs as far as they would go and held them there.

"Lily, I'm going to make love to your pretty pussy with my mouth. I want you to do something for me."

Her pants were audible to her ears. "Yes," she whispered.

"Take your thumbs and index fingers and roll your nipples with them. Do what I would do, rolling, twisting, and tugging."

"Uh—"

"You can do this, Lily. Let me see."

She could do this. Brandon wanted this.

She took her palms and pushed her heavy breasts toward the center of her chest. Then with her thumbs and index fingers she twisted her nipples.

The sensation shot straight down. "Unh."

"Good girl."

She continued and he watched. It was all so erotic. Then he stood before her. "Look at me, Lily. Look what you do to me."

She moaned—the sight of him so impressively hard, and the tingles her every move made on her nipples would soon send her over the edge.

Brandon lowered back down on his knees. His hands on her thighs, he came forward and gently blew a hot breath over her exposed sex. His tongue made one large lap through the center and she nearly flew off the bed.

"Oh, you are so close." He put his whole mouth over the sex and his tongue ran everywhere—into her core, over her lips, and toying with her clit. He lifted his head. "Harder on your nipples, Lily. I want them sore tomorrow."

Oh God. She wanted to come so badly. She twisted and tugged, and as he returned his tongue to her aching clit, she felt the beginnings of a glorious orgasm. He backed off the pressure some, stringing out the climax.

"Ah, Brandon. Ah." He pushed two fingers inside and stroked, and danced his tongue over her clit more.

Her orgasm hit, as fierce as ever.

Fast as lightning, Brandon pulled out his fingers, rammed in his cock, and lifted her thighs higher to meet him standing. His fingers dug into her thighs, but she didn't care.

He pumped and drove to the end, hitting some sweet spot deep inside.

She screamed out as another orgasm hit on the tail of the last one.

A few beats and Brandon was coming too. Growling out her name, before collapsing beside her. They lay there, side by side, panting, sweating, and basking in the glow of some of the best sex in the world.

He threw the condom off to the side, grabbed a blanket from the end of the bed, and covered them. He pulled her close. "You are so beautiful when you come."

"You are so strong."

He chuckled lightly. "Sleep, baby." He kissed her head before they both dozed off in a sexual coma.

Chapter 4

LILY ROLLED OVER and without opening her eyes, she knew the sun was up. Brandon's bed was so comfortable; it cradled her body like a mother holding a baby. She'd slept soundly.

She stretched, feeling the tightness in her muscles, the twinge between her legs, and sighed. Signs of a body that had been well-loved.

She heard rustling and smelled coffee. She opened her eyes to see Brandon setting a steaming cup on her nightstand, dressed for work. He sat on the edge of the bed and leaned down, placing a kiss on her shoulder.

"Good morning, beautiful."

"Good morning, handsome."

"Sleep well?"

"Yes." She smiled. "And you?"

"Best sleep in a long time. I have an early meeting. Help yourself to whatever you want for breakfast. HR isn't expecting you until ten."

She rose to an elbow, and widened her eyes. "Ten? Brandon, I said no preferential treatment."

He held up his hands in surrender. "I did that last week, *before* the ground rules. I knew you would be tired, so I figured a few extra hours would help."

She relaxed her frown. "Okay. Forgiven. Thank you for that," she said sheepishly.

He smiled. "Dinner tonight?"

"Yes."

"Good, and one more thing." He leaned forward, placing a closed-mouth, sweet, long kiss on her lips. "I love you."

She gasped in surprise. He smiled and rose to leave the room. After several seconds, she heard the front door open and close.

Wow! Those three amazing words from Brandon sent her to cloud-nine. A giggle bubbled up. "I love you, too," she told the empty space.

Brandon would have given his eyeteeth to have stayed in bed with Lily this morning. Instead he'd jumped out of bed at six, and by seven he was out the door.

Waking up with her beside him, naked, warm, and beautiful. Truth be told, he awoke around five, but laid beside her, gently touching her skin, listening to her soft breathing. He'd secretly kissed her shoulder, neck, and back a few times. When his cock stirred, he'd stopped. He swore he would not wake her up early, not on her first day of work.

Sometimes, the sex will have to take a backseat.

The idea struck him like a jolt of electricity, something he might have been denying for a long time. He was in love with Lily Bennett.

Once he was certain in his mind, he didn't hesitate to tell her that morning. In fact, he'd relished it. Her expression had been priceless, how her eyes widened and twinkled as a smile crept across her face.

As Gerry pulled up to his office, a short distance away, Brandon felt lighter, in a way he couldn't explain. He looked forward to his dinner with Lily that night, but for now, work awaited. And based on a few early emails, he had some fires to put out too.

His early meeting was with his Director of Research and Development, Roberta, and her second in charge, William Blanken-something, and another researcher, Blanca Flores.

Roberta discussed how R&D had made improvements to Laurel's infusion pumps, ventilators, and dialysis units to minimize alarm fatigue. The team seemed very excited based on the early results from tests performed.

William informed Brandon, "The alarms are designed to warn of potential dangers to patients, but alarms can contribute to adverse events."

Brandon finished his thought. "Like when the appropriate medical personnel aren't alerted."

William seemed impressed that Brandon knew more than a peripheral understanding about the equipment.

His eyes narrowed as something else came to mind. "Roberta, I just want to confirm these changes aren't in response to a serious injury or incident."

"Correct, we've had no reports come back directly about injury from our equipment. But in especially high-volume times, hospitals can get overloaded, mistakes happen. If we can make some small changes, we can likely help on their end."

"Okay, Roberta, William, let's reconvene before we go to the FDA for approval. Good work."

"Thank you, sir."

"What's next on the agenda?"

Roberta glanced at her list. "Blanca, would you like to update us on the drug device combination products?"

"Okay." Blanca reached down into her bag to retrieve a syringe tube-like thing, and set it on the middle of the table. "Mr. Morgan, as you are aware Laurel has been in the drug device combination market for a while. Well, per our goals for the year," she glanced at Roberta quickly, "we are expanding into that realm."

"It is a fast-growing segment," Brandon acknowledged.

She pushed her glasses up the bridge of her nose. "Yes, this device can be coated or impregnated with a drug or biologic for use in hospitals and clinics."

Brandon lifted the contraption to study it closer. Blanca explained how it worked, gave examples of it uses, and told him what the competition was currently selling.

"Impressive. When will this be ready for FDA?"

Roberta chimed in. "We need another month or so. Not long."

"Based on feedback, we have some finessing yet to do, sir," Blanca added.

"Excellent. Keep me posted."

The meeting wrapped after several more minor topics were covered. Randy normally attended those meetings, but had a family emergency that pulled him away. It was clear though that the R&D team was doing a bang-up job.

Brandon returned to his desk to sift through some messages and email.

Donna poked her head through his office doorway. "Sir, you have thirty minutes before your quarter-end meeting. Can I get you anything?

"A glass of ice water would be great. Thank you, Donna."

She paused briefly, as if she hadn't heard him correctly. "Yes, sir."

"And Donna," he made sure to directly connect eye to eye, "when it's just you and I, please call me Brandon."

"Yes, Brandon." She spun around and went for water. She said the words, but as was usually the case, it wouldn't last long. She would likely be calling him *sir* before the end of the day.

Brandon usually asked for coffee in the mornings, but that day, he didn't need it. He felt so good, caffeine wasn't necessary.

Donna arrived with his drink and placed a pitcher of water on the conference table in his office.

After two more meetings, several phone calls, and sifting through email, the morning flew by. Most mornings were like that for Brandon.

Brandon walked out of his office toward the executive dining room hoping to grab some lunch before his two o'clock. He stopped at Donna's desk. "Donna, would you call Bachendorf's, ask them to stay open a little later for me tonight?"

"Yes, sir."

"Thank you." He held back a smile. *Speaking of which . . .* He lifted his cell phone and tapped out a text to the woman he was planning to surprise.

How is your day going so far?

She replied after several seconds.

Good. Crazy. Learning so much. I'll tell you about it tonight.

He smiled.

Great. I'll pick you up at my place at 7:30.

That likely had her confused. Brandon needed it to feel like a date, so that meant any of her preparations were without an audience.

She replied: *OK.*

Brandon had successfully finished his day at five so he could hit the gym on the ground floor, another upgrade from his Miami building. He kept clothes in a closet attached to his office, so after a quick shower and a fresh suit, he rang Gerry for his shopping trip.

Lily's head swam. Her first day with Laurel was incredible *and* overwhelming. The place was so high-tech, and yet had some homely comforts, like a ladies lounge, dimly lit for a quick powernap. *Nice.*

After Lily finished her new hire paperwork, a rep from HR, Leti, showed her around. First, Leti took her to her office on the eighth floor, situated with the Corticelli-transition team. She briefly toured the lunchroom, the gym, and the daycare. They traveled to most floors in the twenty-story building, meeting people key to her position. They never went to the twentieth floor, although Lily wasn't sure how'd she feel about running into Brandon anyway.

Leti merely informed her, "That's Mr. Morgan's office and a few other executive offices. Mr. Morgan is very personable. You'll probably meet him some day, and I'll warn you now." Leti leaned closer conspiratorially. "Try and keep your mouth closed. He's gorgeous."

Leti smiled and nodded with her eyes rounded causing Lily to giggle. What she really wanted to say was *You have no idea.*

At five o'clock, Leti told her she could go and where to report in two days for classroom training on the organization and products Laurel manufactured.

Where did the day go?

She'd traded a few quick texts with Brandon and wondered if she should text him then, but she decided against it. As she sat in a taxi in Dallas rush hour traffic, she mentally walked her closet thinking about what she'd wear for her date with Brandon. She had one great dress in mind—black, body-conscious with a deep-V to show off her cleavage. She had the heels and thigh highs, and a jacket that would be suitable in case the temperature dropped.

Oh yeah. This would be a great date night.

Brandon walked into Bachendorf's jewelers after closing time and was immediately greeted by the manager, a well-groomed, shorter man, slightly graying at the temples with a wide, white smile.

"Mr. Morgan, welcome back. How's your watch?"

Brandon lifted his wrist, revealing a hint of the item. "I love it, Mr Sampson. Excellent timepiece."

Mr. Sampson nodded. "Indeed. So what brings you by today? Something for your mother or sisters?"

"A girlfriend, actually."

Mr. Sampson lifted his brows. "Very well. We have many pieces sure to delight her. Where shall we start?"

Brandon took an entire hour perusing the finest Bachendorf's had to offer. He couldn't not imagine Lily wearing just about anything in the store. By the time his platinum card hit the counter, Brandon had five pieces of jewelry picked out, and even then, he vacillated on a particular necklace.

Mr. Sampson interrupted his thoughts. "Mr. Morgan, if you change your mind about the ruby necklace, I'll happily bring it your office."

That's the reason why he gave his business to Mr. Sampson. Excellent customer service.

He smiled. "Very well. I appreciate the offer. This should do it for today."

With his selections elegantly wrapped, Brandon had thirty minutes to get to his condo and pick up his lovely date.

He wanted it to feel as much as an authentic date as he could, but waiting at his own front door, might be a stretch. He knocked and after a few beats, he entered. Lily was nowhere to be seen.

"My lady," he called out. "Your chariot awaits."

"One moment, kind sir," she called from his bedroom.

He glanced at his empty sofa and took a seat, tapping the box in his jacket pocket. After a few brief moments, she appeared.

Lily had walked down the hall without him noticing. She stood in the entryway to his living room, looking absolutely flawless. Perfect. A vision, the way her dress hugged her breasts and her hips. Shit, his dick could care less about dinner.

He rose. "Lily," he stalked closer to her, "you are breathtaking. That dress looks amazing on you."

"I'm so glad you like it."

He made a full circle around her, inspecting every gorgeous inch. She'd dressed for him. The way she looked at him, with a twinkle in her eye, told him fate had brought him an exceptional woman.

Chapter 5

LILY SHOULD PINCH herself. This handsome prince of a man stood before her, smiling, complimenting her, and just that morning proclaimed that he loved her.

Brandon leaned down and kissed her cheek. "I'm wondering if you might like a little accessory to go with that dress." He reached into his jacket pocket to pull out a small box and popped open the lid, displaying the necklace—a classic heart shape filled with pavé diamonds set in platinum.

She gasped softly. "Oh, Brandon. It's beautiful," she whispered.

He slipped the necklace from the box and clasped it around her neck. Her fingers toyed with the pendant. He brushed her hair aside and brought his lips to her exposed skin. She shivered at his touch.

She spun around and smiled, mist gathering in her eyes. "Thank you." With a hand on his chest she craned her neck and kissed him. "This is incredibly sweet of you."

His smile showed his beautiful white teeth. "You're welcome. Shall we dine?" He presented his elbow.

They arrived at the five-star restaurant with a view of the lights downtown. Brandon's warm hand on her lower back guided her through the elegant, candle-lit restaurant.

The waitress came to take their beverage order and gave an indulgent smile to Brandon as he selected a bottle of white wine and several appetizers. Lily shifted her seat.

The waitress retreated to the kitchen, and he turned his attention to her. "So, how was your first day?"

Before she could answer, his phone rang.

He let out an exasperated sigh. "Cindy. What's up? . . . That's supposed to be in the risk assessment . . . Has Marcus seen it? . . . That would be great. Thank you."

He silenced his phone and tended closer to her. "I'm sorry about that. I thought I shut that thing off."

Brandon was President and Chairman of a major corporation. These kinds of things would crop up and Lily just needed to go with the flow. "It's okay."

"So, I'm anxious to hear. How was your first day?"

Over wine and appetizers, she filled him in on her day and everyone she'd met. "And I can't believe you have a gym in the building."

He grinned.

She had a list of things to find since moving to Texas: a gym, a dry cleaners, a good coffee shop, a dentist, and a gynecologist. But now she had her gym—very convenient.

"Where did they set you up?"

"Eighth floor."

"Great."

She lifted an eyebrow. "Brandon, you can't come to see me there."

"I know."

She narrowed her eyes, not sure if she believed him.

They dined on sumptuous grilled salmon, asparagus, and a light rice pilaf. They chatted as they'd done several times before, although it felt like a million. Talking with Brandon was so easy, so effortless. Since reconnecting with him at his new headquarters in Dallas, spending time together, she felt him slowly opening up, more and more every day. And she loved it.

They declined dessert since she was stuffed. Then out of the blue, she yawned.

He grinned. "Let's call it a night."

"I'm sorry. I think the excitement of the day just wore me out."

She dozed off in the limo, resting her head against Brandon's shoulder.

"We're here, baby," he whispered in her hair.

He wrapped an arm around her waist, supporting her as they walked inside and rode the elevator to his floor.

She fondled her new necklace and images of Brandon at the jewelry store popped in her mind. Shopping for her, only her. Thinking of something special for her. The thoughts made her heart warm. Suddenly, she couldn't sleep. Or perhaps she didn't want to sleep. She wanted to make love to her man.

She left her purse on the dresser, and after locking the front door, Brandon joined her in the bedroom.

"You have a big day tomorrow too. Moving day."

"I do."

"Okay, I'm going to do a bit of work. You head to bed and I'll be in in a while."

Hmm, not so fast.

She presented her back. "Would you please unzip my dress?" She pulled her hair aside and felt the vibration of the zipper going down her back.

She intentionally hadn't bothered to remove her heels. She knew he loved her in high heels. The dress loose, she stepped out of it, and slung it on the bench.

His eyes locked on her body decked in heels, black thigh highs, lacy thong and matching bra.

Her lips curled slightly as she approached him. "Thank you." Then she placed her hands on his chest and leaned in to kiss him.

She started with a sweet kiss, but lingered, allowing one kiss to meld into another. He grasped his hands around her jaw and met her tongue with his. The hardness of his erection pressed into her. She went to work on his shirt buttons when he broke the kiss.

"Lily, we don't—"

"I want to." She reached around to her back and unclasped her bra, dropping it to the floor. "I want you."

He inhaled through clenched teeth. "You look sexy as fuck."

He yanked on his shirt, snapping off the last two buttons. She helped him with his pants. He sat in the chair, jerking off his shoes and socks.

She chuckled at him.

He pulled a condom from the back pocket of his slacks before dumping them in the pile.

She reached for the prophylactic and snatched it from his hand. "Allow me." With a saucy grin, she held the condom wrapper between her teeth, and went to her knees before him.

She itched to feel him in her hands, to caress him. Before she ripped the package, she circled her hand around his cock and stroked up and down, eliciting a low groan from him. She brought her lips close to him and swiped her tongue across the head.

"Shit," he hissed out.

In tandem with her fist, she worked him up and down—sucking and licking. As much as she enjoyed pleasuring Brandon, as usual, she received pleasure too. A wetness began to gather at the apex of her thighs.

His hands clasped the sides of her head. "Lily. Sweetheart."

She released him with a *pop*, and looked up into his eyes. "I want to be inside you," he said with a growl to his voice.

She slipped the condom from its wrapper and sheathed him. Then she stood before him, and ever so slowly dragged her thong to the floor and stepped out of it.

"Are you wet?" he asked, his eyes dark as the night sky.

"Why don't you find out?"

He smirked at her new-found sassiness, and slid his fingers up her thigh, stopping at his destination. With a single finger he dragged through her slit, sending sensations to every cell in her body.

"Oh yes."

She cupped her hands on his shoulders. "Well, then that should be it for the preliminaries, Mr. Morgan." Braced, she carefully lifted one leg, bent at the knee, and wove it under the arm of his chair. She did the same with her other leg, straddling him. Forced to sit on his lap, her pussy mere inches from his cock, eager to connect with him.

He laid his hands on her hips as she fisted him and hitched up enough to align herself with him. Slowly, she slid down over him, savoring the push against her vaginal walls. She let her head fall back and moaned.

He dug his fingers into her flesh. "You are a beautiful sight. My wanton woman."

She rocked on him. "Oh, Brandon. It's so much deeper this way."

"Yes, baby. Take your time."

She moved. "Oh, God. So incredible."

"We have all night, beautiful." He slid his hands reverently over her necklace, to her breasts. Lifting her closer to his mouth, he sucked in a nipple. He nipped with his teeth and the sensation shot straight to her clit.

"Unh," she called out.

He tormented her second breast the same, triggering the slow beginnings of her climax.

"Brandon."

He lifted his head to gaze straight into her eyes. She moved with him, peering deep into the soul of the man who brought her so much joy. "I love you."

He grabbed her face with two hands. "I love you, too, Lily." He crashed his lips to hers, joining them further. She pulled herself even closer and rode him harder.

"Fuck, Lily."

"Ah," she cried out as her climax hit with maximum intensity, and that only sparked his.

He wrapped two strong arms around her pumping one last time before releasing all the tension in his muscles. She loved how satisfied he became after making love.

They smiled at each other, and said no words. With his help, she maneuvered out of the chair. He rose and pulled on some sweatpants and a t-shirt. She wrapped herself in a robe and padded to the bathroom to get ready for bed. He followed her.

"I need to get some work done. Okay?"

"Yes, I'll see you in bed later," she said with a smile. She would not be some needy girlfriend, holding him back from running *a company*, no less.

He pecked her cheek, then her lips. "See you soon." Then he spun around, heading to his home office.

She glanced at her image in the mirror. Perfectly disheveled hair, pouty, swollen lips, flushed cheeks. A definite FF look—freshly fucked. She giggled at herself, grabbed her toothbrush, and started her bedtime routine.

Life couldn't get much better.

Chapter 6

LILY WAS ANTSY with excitement waiting for the movers to arrive.

That morning, Brandon had finagled her out of tank top and boxer shorts to have his wicked way with her. Then he'd kissed her soundly, wished her luck on her move, and headed to the office.

She'd packed what little she had at Brandon's, lugged it to a waiting taxi, and took the twenty-minute drive to her new apartment.

She was able to get some shelf liner down when, finally, the van arrived. It took little time to get her stuff off the truck, and then her real work began.

Her new place was mostly neutral—grays and beiges. She knew without a doubt she'd need to work in some color. She didn't do blah. The carpet looked pretty new, and granite countertops were added to the kitchen. The bathroom hadn't been updated, but it was big and clean, and that's all she cared about, really. She would be spending a lot of time at Brandon's and in Rome for the Corticelli transition.

She stopped a few times—to eat some leftovers she'd hijacked from Brandon's fridge, and to answer an email from her mom. That afternoon, Brandon texted.

How's moving day?

She smiled just thinking of him

Great. Movers left. Unpacking boxes now. How is your day?

He replied a moment later.

Boring without you around. Come over for dinner tonight.

She grinned. It's not like she could see him at work anyway.

OK. Cya tonight. XX

When all her clothes were unpacked, she moved to the bathroom to organize her toiletries. *Hm, I should think about having duplicates at Brandon's. The chance that he'll let me sleep here all the time is slim to none.* She chuckled. Not that she *wanted* to sleep there every night. By herself.

She had just enough time to finish laying the shelf liner in the kitchen cabinets before she'd need to get ready to head to Brandon's. Her phone rang. *Courtney.*

"Hey Court. How's it going?"

"Great. How 'bout yourself? Getting all your crap put away?"

She laughed. "Yes. Almost done. But this place is bigger, so I'll need to do some shopping soon."

"Oh, yeah. Well, guess what? The airline's having a sale for October. I want to buy a ticket to come out and visit you. Maybe we can do some shopping then too."

Lily could hear her grin over the phone. "Awesome, sounds like a plan."

Lily opened her calendar app, and went over the dates she was expected in Rome. There were two good weekends; any other weekend, and their time would get cut short.

"I'll check out the flights and get back to you. Oh, I'm so excited. I've never been to Dallas."

"We can discover it together."

The ladies talked and laughed a while longer, until Courtney dropped off so Lily could get back to work. She was able to get more of her kitchen in order, before heading for the shower. She wanted to look and smell good for dinner with her boyfriend.

Shit! He was running late. Brandon hated being late. He called the doorman's desk at his condo building, asking Andrew to let Lily into his place. He happily agreed.

His meeting with Marcus, his VP of Finance, ran long. It, of course, was a productive meeting, and they covered quarter-end figures, year-end estimates, and Corticelli financials.

Brandon stopped the meeting as it had already gone over, and had Donna schedule another meeting with Marcus for later in the week.

He glared at his to-do list. Why did he feel like he had a crazy-damn day and yet got very little accomplished?

"Let's go!" he yelled at the rush hour traffic. He glanced at the clock. After seven. He'd texted Lily from the office to let her know he was running behind. She'd replied, *OK.*

When he arrived, she looked completely at home on his living room sofa, completely desirable in her slim-fitting blue jeans and cream, breast-hugging sweater with her new necklace barely licking at her cleavage. Just where he wanted to lick.

Her head raised from looking at her phone, and she smiled. He divested himself of his tie and jacket and knelt before her.

He placed a simple kiss on her lips, and she cupped his cheek. "Forgive me."

"Forgiven. How was your day?"

"A crazy one. How was yours?"

"Good. A bit exhausting. I have more to do over the next few days, including shopping, but it will be fine."

He was glad she was happy, though he secretly envisioned her at his place—day and night—but happy nevertheless. "Are you hungry?"

She nodded. "Famished."

He kissed her beautiful plump lips again, stood, and offered her a hand. "I think we have salmon in here."

Sure enough, just as his cook had promised. In his refrigerator sat a scrumptious-looking, pink salmon filet in a glass pan ready to bake. He lifted the card, reading the instructions to preheat the oven.

"It looks like we have rice and veggies, too."

"What can I do?" she asked.

"How about going to the wine fridge and pulling out a nice white?"

She made a step and paused. "Brandon, I need to confess, I know little about wine."

He grinned. He relished the idea of teaching her about wine. "Well, either a sauvignon blanc or a chardonnay will work great with the fish. So how about you pick one of those."

She smoothed her lips together and nodded.

Whatever she chose, he would love. As she was distracted he heard his phone vibrate in his suit jacket pocket. He checked it. Nothing that couldn't wait until morning.

They worked together, side by side, making dinner. She told about her cooking experience—some things were excellent and some would take more practice, she shared.

"Okay, so what dishes do you make well?"

"I make an insane omelet," she said as they sat at his dining table.

His brows lifted.

"Uh-huh. And spaghetti and meatballs." The pride in her smile made her look adorable. He wanted to lean in and kiss her.

"Well, you can make those for us sometime."

The conversation continued as they devoured dinner. She spoke more about her new place, and invited him to *come over sometime.*

"I'd love to see it."

As they finished dinner, Lily confessed, "Brandon, I'm beat."

"You've had a big day. I'll clean up here, why don't you go get ready for bed? I'll meet you shortly."

Her eyes crinkled at the edges as she smiled. "You are a nice man, Mr. Morgan."

"Thank you, Miss Bennett."

She sidled past the table and down the hall to the bathroom.

He resisted the urge to grab his phone or the Journal, which was his norm most nights at home. He made it a priority to keep up with his company, his people, the industry, and the economy. All the aspects that played into the success of Laurel and its future.

After he stacked most of the dishes, soaked the oven pan, and put the last of the wine in the fridge, he felt satisfied that a *huge* mess didn't await his housekeeper in the morning. Now to find the woman of his dreams.

He grabbed his half-full wineglass and strode into the bedroom. His eyes immediately went to a sleeping Lily in his bed. The corners of his lips lifted. Her breathing was deep and steady. She was exhausted.

He walked to her side of the bed, tended toward her, and placed a gently kiss on her forehead.

Mine.

He turned off the lamp on the dresser, darkness falling in the room. He'd have to wait to be naked in bed with his beauty. Instead, he grabbed his phone and headed to his home office to get some work done.

Hours passed when Brandon realized it was midnight. He felt productive, accomplished.

He quietly closed the bathroom door to do his business and get ready for bed. Then he slid in between the covers and pulled Lily's warm form into his.

He could definitely get used to a life like this.

Chapter 7

"I'D LIKE TO sleep at my place tonight. How about you come over?" she told him with a grin the next morning.

"Alright. I can do that."

"Now, I need to get to work. Lots to learn," she announced when he reached for her, but she was too quick. "Sorry, no shenanigans this morning, love. But . . ." her voice pitched higher, "I have a surprise for you tonight." She gave him a quick peck on the lips.

He chuckled. "I can't wait."

And before he could convince her to reconsider going to work early, she'd dashed into the bathroom and blasted the shower.

Tonight. He could be patient.

Lily got settled at her desk and buzzed Leti.

"Hey, you're in early," Leti said in greeting.

"G'morning. How about we grab a coffee? I have a few questions before we get started."

"Great idea. You wanna come to five and I'll make a fresh pot? I bought French Vanilla creamer."

She heard Leti's smile over the phone. "Yum. I'll be right there."

The rest of the day ran by in a blur. At times, Lily questioned if she could keep up. The rest of the week and the following week was laid out for her. Leti handed her the organizational chart including department overviews, and flight itinerary to Rome, which she'd been expecting. Classes on products started Monday. Leti made it clear that she wasn't expected to know this stuff right off the bat, and it would come in time.

Yeah, well, Lily generally felt more confident in her role if she knew all she could, as quickly as she could.

"Alright, you had a great day. Go home. See your boyfriend or call him or whatever," Leti said with a devilish grin.

"Uh, there will be none of that."

"What? You don't have a boyfriend?"

Oops! She was not prepared for this conversation. "We just started dating, so . . . I don't really want to talk about it yet."

"Afraid you'll jinx it?" Leti grinned.

She smiled back at the woman she quickly felt a growing connection with. "Yeah, something like that."

"Okay, well, have a great night. I'll see you tomorrow." Leti spun around on the ball of her foot and headed toward the elevator.

Yes, a great night indeed.

She exhaled and thanked the angels above that the necklace Brandon had given her was hidden beneath her ruffle-front blouse.

Lily had time to pick up groceries, a bottle of wine, and a lighter on her way to her new apartment. Her place wasn't *nearly* as nice as Brandon's, but given some time, she would make it feel cozy, make it feel like home.

Her dish was a simple, but delicious, orange chicken recipe. After she set everything in the oven, she made her way to the shower. With thirty minutes before Brandon was expected, she finished her makeup, spritzed her hair, and lit a few candles.

The doorbell rang, and her heart skipped a beat. She opened the door to her handsome man, standing before her wearing a sexy grin, holding a bouquet of red roses. She could still pinch herself. That this sexy, smart, successful man wanted her- "Middle-America" Lily.

"Hello, handsome. Come in."

"Hello, beautiful." He leaned forward to kiss her cheek, and handed her the flowers.

What a gentleman.

"Thank you. Please come in."

"Nice place."

She snorted. "How can you say that?" She motioned with her hand. "Stacks of boxes, no artwork on the walls, and zero color."

"You are all the color this place needs." His lips curled as he slipped off his suit jacket and tie.

She pointed a finger at him. "Ah, flattery will get you everywhere."

He came up behind her, grasped her hips, and kissed her neck. "I hope so," he whispered.

50

She smiled to herself. "Dinner needs a few more minutes. Would you like a glass of wine?" She pivoted to face him.

"Sure, but when do I get this surprise you promised me?"

"After dinner. Patience, Mr. Morgan."

His eyes turned an unfathomable deep espresso. "I've waited months for you, Lily. And I was with no one while you were gone. You were all I wanted. All I want."

Oh God. His words warmed her to the core, and yet a ping of guilt punched her in the gut. He had waited *for her*. And all the time, she'd ached for him.

She moved closer. "I waited for you, too." She raised an inch on her toes to kiss him sweetly. His palm closed around the back of her neck, taking the kiss deeper. Something more heated.

This man could turn her insides to gelatin.

She pulled back before they got completely distracted from dinner. "Brandon, I want to cook for you."

The smile lit up his entire face. "I'd love that. My mother loves to cook too."

"She does?" Lily reached for wine glasses and the corkscrew.

"Yes. We have a cook most days, but Sundays, in particular, were for family dinners and she'd cook."

Of course, they have a cook.

She glanced at his solemn face as she handed him a glass of wine. "Do you miss your mom?"

"I do. Maybe someday, we can take a trip to Miami and visit them."

The sincere way he said it—the way he held her eyes—she knew he meant it. He wanted to introduce her to his parents. How thrilling and unsettling at the same time.

"Let's eat." A change of subject would be good. So much heavy conversation, when all she wanted was a quiet night with Brandon in her arms.

Over dinner he quizzed her about her day. She had so much to tell him. When the subject of going to Rome came up, he pouted. It was uncharacteristically Brandon. And adorable.

"It will only be for two weeks."

He grunted. "Let me know if they give you any trouble."

Seriously? "I'll be fine."

Dinner turned out good, and she was pleased.

"That was delicious, Lily."

"Thank you."

They cleaned up and the fizz of anticipation started to build. She was sure he could feel it too.

"If you'd follow me, please."

Her white teeth flashed at him as she took his hand and led him to the bedroom.

She turned on a bedside table lamp and soft light barely made it to the corners of the room. Brandon didn't care. There was enough light to see what he wanted-Lily.

She pulled him to the bed and he sat. Her lips glazed over his, soft and kissable. "I actually have two surprises for you."

He lifted an eyebrow. "Really?"

She stepped back and slowly undressed herself, shedding an article of clothing, one piece at a time. Until she wore only black satin and lace bra and panties. She looked incredibly fuckable. He shifted in his seat, adjusting his growing erection.

Continuing her striptease, she eased her bra off, letting it fall to the carpet. He held back the need to lunge at her and taste her gorgeous, full breasts.

Slowly, his eyes adjusted to the dim light, and for that he was thankful, because the last piece to go were her panties. Lily hooked her thumbs under the waistband and dragged them to the floor. When she stood, he gasped. She'd completely shaven herself.

He looked up at her face, saw the tentative smile on her lips.

He motioned her closer with the flick of two fingers. With his hands at her hips, he stared, awed really, at her beautiful pussy. He slid his fingertips over her freshly revealed skin and sucked in a breath. She moaned.

"Lily, I love it." He stroked using both hands, and as she widened her stance, he glossed over her lips. His cock grew. He was rock-hard with wanting her.

He glanced up, her lips parted and her face flush, waiting for his next move. "This is so fucking beautiful. I'm going to make love to your exquisite pussy with my mouth. Please lie down."

As she settled in the middle of the bed, he stripped out of his fucking clothes as fast as he could. Too many damn clothes.

He walked to the bed looking down her; she watched his every move. Hands straddling her face, he lowered himself to kiss her deeply, claiming her, grateful for his wonderful gift.

Then he moved his kisses to her beautiful tits, sucking hard on her pointed nipples until she cried out. He straightened, grabbed her legs just above her knees and dragged her to the edge of the bed.

She shrieked in surprise. He dropped to his knees, pushed her legs apart, and lay claim to his.

"Ah!" she yelled, bending her head back.

She was slick with wetness, hot and ready for him. Ready for him to make her come. Ready for him to drive into her. He wanted to hear her scream his name over and over.

She moaned with his every move.

He licked up her luscious milk, pressing into her channel, circling her clit. Over and over, he teased her, tasted her, and loved driving her out of her mind.

He pushed her legs further apart and suckled her clit, followed by pressing his tongue and massaging it.

"Unh."

He pressed his lips onto her soft pure skin and, with his tongue flattened, he drove her over the edge.

"Brandon!" She arched her back, her head thrashed back and forth a few times before the tremors subsided.

He pulled a condom from his pants' pocket and ripped open the package.

"Wait," she called to him.

He startled.

She pushed herself upright and took the package out of his hand, tossing it to the floor.

He wrinkled his brow.

"Brandon, that's my other surprise. I'm on the pill. It's been seven days, so now we don't need any other form of protection."

Was he hearing her right? He could go bareback. He never—ever—went bareback. It was like the Holy Grail.

"Oh, damn, Lily." He cupped her cheek, and bent forward to kiss her. He wrapped an arm around her and hauled her back to the center of the bed. He dragged his kisses to her sweet neck, gently positioning himself between her. With her legs hooked around his waist and her arms around his neck, he pushed his head inside her wet, warm channel.

"Oh fuck, Lily." He paused; the sensation overwhelmed him and nearly had him blowing his seed. He pushed inside her fully and froze. "You feel amazing," he breathed over her lips. His heart jackhammered in his chest.

"So do you."

She rained kisses on his lips, cheeks, and neck. He started to move again. *Fucking insane.*

"Lily," he panted, "I've never done this before . . . skin to skin. God. I don't know how long I can last."

With her hands on his jaw, she looked at him straight in the eyes, like they were the only two people on the planet. "Fuck me, Brandon."

He growled and moved, driving harder each push, faster each pull. He kept his eyes locked on hers, and hers on him. He'd never made love like this before. He wanted this forever.

"Lily, I love you." *Push.* "I am so fucking crazy for you." The bed creaked.

"Ah!" Her eyes closed briefly. She was close. "I'm crazy for you."

He locked his lips to hers and drove both of them to the heart of ecstasy. She screamed into his mouth and he savored every last moment.

Sliding out of his love, he collapsed beside her and pulled her in close. His chest rose and fell in recovery.

"Best. Present. Ever."

Chapter 8

LILY CONTEMPLATED HER first two weeks at Laurel. What a whirlwind!

She'd started a new job, reconnected with Brandon, moved halfway across the country, and now she sat in first class on her way to Rome.

She was so happy, she could cry.

The thought of going back to Italy had seemed out of reach. Naturally, this trip also entailed a bunch of new responsibilities. She was nervous but excited too. Brandon had faith in her, he told her so. She needed to leverage that and muster a bit more confidence to tackle this new chapter.

Corticelli Labs was officially a Laurel subsidiary.

Lily learned from the transition team that the purchase was perceived as "friendly". She also learned that keeping high employee retention meant Corticelli employees must feel like they could continue doing their jobs without affecting their independence.

Brandon said as much. *Get the pulse of the employees, Lily. I need to know if they're thinking about leaving?*

She wanted desperately to make him proud of her. She did not want to let him down.

Lily was greeted a few hours later at da Vinci-Fiunicino airport by a short, smiling woman named Emma.

"Hello. Welcome to Roma." Her eyes twinkled when she smiled.

"Hello. Thank you."

"I'm to take you to your hotel, Casa Montani, and return in the morning to pick you up." Her English was quite good. "Tomorrow, I will give you a tour and you will meet the transition team." She looked up at Lily as they walked to her little yellow car. "We are very excited to see you."

"Yes?"

"Oh yes." Emma's eyes rounded. "We heard that some people might need to move to the United States. Also, we understand Laurel gives end-of-year bonuses." Her grin widened. "And I've seen pictures of the president, Michael Morgan. He is *very* handsome."

This woman was simply a warm bundle of joy. Lily wondered if she ever had a bad day.

"Well, I'm not sure about the first two things, but as for the last, yes, Mr. Morgan *is* handsome."

"Mmm. Have you ever met him?"

"Yes, I have."

"Oh, you are so lucky. He looks *delizioso*."

You have no idea. She smiled back at the woman.

Emma drove her to the hotel. Lily had chosen a different hotel for this trip. The one she'd stayed at when she met Brandon, well, that would always be special. If she returned, it would be with Brandon. She hid her smile as she glanced out the window.

Emma chattered on about this and that. Lily learned that Emma had worked for Corticelli since she'd graduated from college. She had two younger brothers she referred to as *irritante*. And she adored American food, bacon cheeseburgers being her favorite. Lily's lips curved.

"So, how long have you worked for Laurel Medical?"

"Not very long. I was hired to help with the transition. I used to work for a company that owned farms in Italy, so I came here quite frequently."

"Oh, really?" Emma glanced at Lily with surprise.

"Yes, Rome is a great eating town." She wiggled her eyebrows for effect. "La Fraschetta del Pesce and Trattoria der Pallaro are some of my favorites. And Antica Forno Roscioli bakery for pastries and rolls."

Emma flashed her a smile, perhaps not expecting a foreigner who was so familiar with her country. "*Meraviglioso!* Well, if you haven't been to La Locanda del Tempio near the Pantheon, I would like to take you."

"That sounds perfect." Lily had the distinct feeling she and Emma were becoming fast friends. And Lily certainly had room in her life for more of those.

This visit was crucial for Laurel. Most of the transition team from the US would eventually make a trip to Rome to get to know their counterparts, learn more about transacting business in Italy, and understand more about their processes. Lily wasn't responsible for interactions at that level.

Her first meeting—this first meeting—would set the tone. She needed to impart confidence in the Corticelli employees that Laurel was excited about this new partnership. She had several priorities. First, make sure Corticelli retained its unique culture. And secondly, to ensure they didn't lose sight of the relationships they'd built with customers, suppliers, and patients.

Emma parked in front of the hotel. She pulled out a binder from the backseat and handed it to Lily.

"We thought you'd like to have an overview of Corticelli."

Some overview. The thing was three inches thick, but really exactly what Lily wanted. She smiled. "Thanks."

"I will pick you up in the morning. Sleep well." Emma steered her tiny yellow car, that suited her sunny personality, out into traffic.

Lily settled into her clean, bright hotel room. Spread around the king-sized bed, she scanned through the stack of documents. She studied their org chart, especially their transition team, which felt very similar to Laurel's. The binder contained product overviews, the total manufacturing integration overview, industrial policies, a whole host of rules and regulations for corporations conducting business in Italy, and some advanced data analytics.

Holy hell! Her head spun. There was even a document that addressed cyber threats, just like Laurel's. These people were serious.

I guess you have to be.

There was an overview document labeled Products, Services, and R&D. They'd enclosed several white papers on nanotechnology.

The more she read the more questions she had. And she'd barely made a dent.

She rubbed her eyes and let out a sigh.

Her phone dinged with a message.

Brandon texted her: *Good night. Sweet dreams.*

It was ten-thirty, three-thirty in Dallas. She opted to call instead of replying to his text.

"Hey, stranger."

"Hey. How are you?"

"I'm good. Lily, you sound tired. Are you alright?"

She smiled a little smile. "Yes. I am tired. I need to wrap it up. Reading about Corticelli is like reading up on Laurel. There is so much to know."

"Drinking from a firehose."

"Yes." She knew he understood. He may have been born into this business but he knew, for someone outside of the field especially, it could be overwhelming.

"Take it slow. There is no rush for you to learn everything. Goodness, I still don't know it all." She heard his sigh. "Take your time, baby. You're doing great, and I am so proud of you."

"Thanks, Brandon."

"Well, I need to drop off. I have a meeting. Get some rest and I'll call you tomorrow."

"Okay. Thanks. I love you."

"I love you too. 'Night," and the line disconnected.

I am so proud of you. Lily smiled as she continued to stare at her phone. His words touched her more than if he was sitting next to her.

A yawn snuck up on her. With jet lag setting in, she knew anymore time spent reading would be a waste.

She stacked the papers back on the desk and quickly brushed her teeth and washed her face. She set her phone alarm and dozed off instantly. She dreamed of Brandon, whispering in her ear, telling her he was proud of her and that he loved her.

***

Only one day had passed and he already ached for Lily. How the hell was he going to survive a full two weeks without her?

Tuesday morning Brandon arrived at the office before Donna, eager to get to work.

He dumped his leather bag on the credenza and turned on his PC. He could really use a cup of coffee. He hadn't slept the best last night without Lily next to him.

He opened a browser and typed: *flower shops in Rome, Italy.*

Ah-ha!

He picked up the phone and dialed.

"*Ciao.*"

"*Ciao. Parli Inglese?*" he asked the chipper woman on the other end of the line.

"Yes. How can I help you?"

"I would like to order flowers and deliver them to . . ." he glanced at the note in the cell phone, "Casa Montani."

"Certainly."

The woman helped him with his selection and a note card.

Mission accomplished.

Donna walked in with a cup of hot, delicious smelling coffee just as he hung up the phone.

"Ah. Excellent. Thank you, Donna."

He gulped some coffee before setting it down.

"And this just arrived for you." She handed him a return on investment report.

"Thanks."

"And here are a few messages." She placed them in the center of his desk. "Your first meeting is at nine on sixteen. And remember lunch is at Del Frisco's with Dennis Whitehead."

Whitehead was the vice-chair of Laurel's board of directors. He was an organized, detail-oriented, old-school businessman, who liked to meet every quarter with Brandon. Partially, Brandon knew, for business; the other part, to be seen. Dennis loved to be seen rubbing elbows with the business elite. Brandon also knew Dennis was in town from Miami to meet with the chairperson from Frisco Foods. They had a vacancy on their board and Dennis likely wanted a chance at it.

He smiled. "Thanks, Donna."

"You're welcome." She paused another moment in silence.

He glanced up. "Is there something else?"

Her eyes softened and she took a step closer. In a low voice, she said, "Are you gonna get through these two weeks?"

Holy hell! How did she know?

As if reading his mind, she tipped her hand. "I know. I've known how miserable you were when you came back from Rome. I've watched how happy you've been since she interviewed with the company and started working here."

He grinned. Donna knew just about everything regarding him and the company. "I see. Well, do you know I just sent her flowers?"

Donna batted the air with her hand. "Oh, just a matter of time." She spun around and headed to her office. He chuckled at her confidence. Donna was a gem, no doubt about it.

Next item of business, call Leena and see how things were going in Miami. These next two weeks would be chock-full of meetings and conference calls, and anything to keep his mind off Lily. The best thing he could hope for was for the weeks to fly by.

Chapter 9

AFTER EMMA AND Lily filled up extra-large coffee cups with cappuccino, the tour of the corporate offices began. It didn't take too long, and the manufacturing tour would happen later. Lily was anxious to meet the transition team.

Lily sucked in several deep breaths, smoothed her lips together, and followed Emma into a conference room. Lily ignored her racing heart and focused on one face at a time. Emma made introductions of the team, including an accountant, a lawyer, a manager from manufacturing, and two people from the finance department. Lily smiled and kept eye contact, but she could already feel animosity drifting off a few people.

Things were about to get interesting.

"Grazie per il vostro saluto affettuoso. Non vedo l'ora di lavorare con lei. Laurel è molto entusiasta di questa acquisizione."

More than a few eyebrows lifted as Lily greeted them in her flawless Italian.

"I understand you are all fluent in English, so if you don't mind, I'd like to give that a try."

That gained her a few laughs, the loudest from Emma.

"I understand a teleconference call has already been scheduled with the US transition team. But I'm here to get an overview of how you operate and what it is that makes this company so successful."

"How long will you be here?" asked a man to her right.

The question seemed a little off track. Lily noticed the man was taking notes; perhaps they recorded minutes during every meeting.

"I will be here for two weeks."

"Thank you."

She nodded. "Over the next two weeks we will have some one-on-one meetings. Feel free to ask questions at any time." She reached into her suit jacket pocket and retrieved her new business cards. "And you can also get in touch with me through email."

Emma circled the conference table, handing everyone her card.

"There are two big things I need your help with. Laurel doesn't want to change the unique culture you have here at Corticelli. Maintaining that is paramount to keep morale high and prevent unnecessary attrition. And second, we want to ensure folks don't lose sight of the relationships you've built with customers, suppliers, and patients."

"You don't have to worry about that. Everyone loves us because we do the right thing by our customers," a gentleman at the far end piped up.

"And doctors love us because our products save their patients' lives." He leaned back in his chair on one hip, legs crossed, tapping a pen on the corner of the table.

And the first bomb has been lobbed.

Lily took a moment to recall his name and position.

"Riccardo, that is excellent to hear, and as a manager in manufacturing I bet you take pride in making a quality product." She shrugged a shoulder. "Laurel doesn't expect that to change. You've done an outstanding job here, which is exactly what appealed to Laurel when they made the offer to buy."

Riccardo seemed to relax a bit. Lily knew not everyone had looked forward to this merger as Emma had proclaimed, and Lily suspected that was not the last she'd hear from Riccardo.

The rest of the meeting went without much incident. A grumble or two from Riccardo and Umberto, a corporate attorney, otherwise nothing out of the ordinary.

Lily continued to refer to Laurel as *they*. At least for the first few days, she needed to be looked on as a liaison. Someone who could go back to Laurel and represent *their* best interests. By the end of the trip, that would change to *we*.

Lily wanted to collapse. She'd order dinner in her room, because there was no way in hell she was leaving her hotel. The day had been crazy, and productive, and exhausting.

After a moment fumbling with her keycard, she pushed the hotel door open and the sight of two dozen, long-stem red roses immediately welcomed her.

Brandon.

She dropped her bag and keycard on the dresser, then walked to the beautiful bouquet. She pulled the card from its envelope.

The more I think of you, the more I love you, and the more I miss you. Brandon

Aw! What a sweet man!

How did she get so lucky to have this wonderful man in her life?

She texted him immediately.

I love the flowers! Thank you! Long day ended with a big smile when greeted by your beautiful bouquet. xx Lily

She didn't expect a response right away because the chance that Brandon was in the middle of something was probable.

Kicking off her shoes, Lily went to the desk to peruse the room service menu. She considered splurging a little, maybe some meaty lasagna or a seafood pasta dish in a butter sauce.

She called and placed her food order, and began to lay out her schedule for the next two weeks. Most meetings were one-on-ones with members of the transition team, some might include a few employees from the same department. She would take them out to breakfast and lunch, away from the office. Except Riccardo. He would give her a plant tour.

For Friday, Brandon had scheduled a quick *hello* for her with Gian Esposito, the current CEO, soon to be retiring. Sure, no pressure.

Speak of the devil, her phone rang.

"Hello, handsome."

"Hello, beautiful. How's it going?"

"Good. Overall people are receptive to the merger, er, acquisition."

"That's good. So not everyone, huh?"

"No, but they'll come around." She sighed. "Hey, I do have to clarify two things."

"Okay."

"Apparently there is a rumor that some people may move to the States. And next, there is a rumor about year-end bonuses."

Brandon chuckled, and the sound moved over her like a warm blanket. "Well, the official response is bonuses are based on how well the company performs as a whole, so both companies' financials will now be factored into that equation. And two, at this time Laurel sees no need to relocate employees based in Italy to the US."

"Wow. There are bonuses," she whispered.

"Sure. Did your previous employer not do bonuses?"

"Nope, at least not at my level."

"Well, that's a shame. But lucky for me you were on the market." She could hear his smile over the phone.

"Lucky for both of us."

"I miss you. The bed is cold without you."

"I miss you too." She subconsciously held the phone closer.

A knock came at her door.

"Hey, Brandon. My food is here."

"Okay, but keep me on the phone."

Oh, she liked this protective side of Brandon.

She opened the door to a young man wearing black pants and vest and a white long-sleeved shirt. *"Ciao, Signorina* Bennett."

"*Si prega di impostare laggiu.*" She pointed to the small table in the corner. Then she retrieved a few euros from her purse and handed it to him. "*Grazie.*"

"*Prego.*" He smiled and closed the door behind him.

In that sexy voice Brandon sometimes had, he said, "I love to hear you speak Italian."

"Really? I'll be sure to remember that."

"Oh, yes, indeed. Well, I'll let you eat, and I've got work to do. Let's talk tomorrow."

"Okay. Good night. I love you."

"Sweet dreams, love."

She sighed as she looked at her phone. These two weeks were going to be grueling in more ways than one. Her hand absently went to her heart necklace. She already missed his smile first thing in the morning, and the way his arms wrapped around her making her feel safe.

But she was there to do a job, and she wouldn't take it lightly.

Digging into her Italian roulade steak, she moaned aloud. God, she missed this country. A foodie's paradise. Each bite practically melted in her mouth.

She scooted her plate aside and pried open the lid on her laptop.

Laurel had a formal business plan outlining goals, priorities and strategies for a successful transition. She opened that first to review.

Documents had already been combed over by Laurel—everything from financial statements to customer lists to intellectual property rights. Lily was responsible for the people-element—keeping morale high to prevent lost business or headcount.

Her priorities for the evening were one: set up breakfast and lunch appointments, and of course a manufacturing tour, with the transition team members. And two: power through more of the binder so she could get a feel for the structure and the culture of Corticelli, and have questions ready for when she met with everyone.

Then, she could collapse in bed, hopefully get more than eight hours of sleep, and not dream about the sexy, generous man she'd left back in the States.

Chapter 10

LILY HOISTED HER luggage off the conveyor belt at DFW airport when she heard her phone chime.

She stared down at the screen and her jaw dropped reading Brandon's text.

Your plane has landed. Come to my office immediately.

He *commanded* her to come to his office. She should be mad that he was ordering her around like a golden retriever, instead a little buzz ran through her veins.

At almost four o'clock in the afternoon, she knew her coworkers weren't expecting to see her until the next day. She wanted to head to her apartment. After two weeks away, nothing felt better than being home.

She gave the cab driver Laurel's office address.

Smiling, Lily glanced out the car window. She was secretly thrilled to see Brandon. She missed him terribly. He filled her dreams at night, and their texts and phone calls only got her so far. She pulled out a mirror to check her hair and refresh her makeup.

Wait! Was that text in boss-mode or boyfriend-mode? Oh, God, had something gotten back to Brandon about Corticelli that made him mad? She had no idea what Brandon was like mad.

Everything had gone well in Rome, considering. Several people were nervous about keeping their jobs, a few were concerned because they were up for promotions, and one woman in customer service would go on maternity leave and wanted to be sure she could come back to the job she loved. Nothing Lily couldn't handle. Even Riccardo and Umberto seemed pleasant to her at the end of the two weeks.

She nibbled her lips so much, she was sure her lipstick was gone. Her hands felt sweaty.

The cab dropped her in front of the building. She strode onto the elevator, feeling like a moron with her luggage in tow, and punched twenty.

Donna smiled when Lily approached.

"Hi, Donna."

"Hi, Lily. Nice to see you again."

"Mr. Morgan wanted to see me right away."

"Yes, follow me."

Donna opened the door. "Mr. Morgan, Lily is here. And my apologies, I have a doctor's appointment. I need to leave early," she announced.

She smiled again at Lily and briskly left, closing the door behind her.

Lily planted her feet, watching Brandon cross from behind his desk. She swallowed. His mere presence both calmed and excited her. He was so handsome in suit pants, crisp shirt and tie. She desperately wanted to jump into his arms. But she was so baffled by his text, she didn't know what to expect.

"I came right away, Mr. Morgan." She heard the hesitancy in her own voice.

He shook his head.

"Brandon?"

He nodded.

That was all she needed to know. She dropped her purse and let go of her luggage handle, and ran to him. He pulled her into a warm embrace and crushed his firm lips onto hers. Her arms wrapped around his neck, as he lifted her to her toes, holding her closer to him.

She broke for only a second to gasp a breath. "I missed you so much."

His kiss was hungry and passionate, as he plumbed her depths. She moaned when he released her, only to hold her nape and nibble on her ear. "You have no idea how much I missed you," he whispered against her neck.

His tongue skated across her skin, sending shivers throughout her body. Her breasts grew heavy and she longed to have him touch her, but they couldn't, not here.

He pulled back, locking her in a penetrating stare that instantly had her flushed.

"Take off your blouse." His husky voice, rich with lust.

Her jaw dropped.

He circled around her to lock his office door.

She shook her head weakly in protest. "We can't, Brandon . . ."

His hands yanked off his tie and began unbuttoning his shirt. He held her gaze.

"The rules. Remember the rules?"

"Fuck the rules. This is my company." He dropped his shirt and reached for hers, tugging it out of her pants' waistband.

She watched, frozen in bewilderment, as he slipped off her blouse. The apex of her thighs ached and dampness collected on her panties.

He moved closer, grabbing her hands, kissing her palms and wrists. "If I want to fuck my girlfriend on my office desk after she's been gone for two weeks, I will."

"But—"

He stealthily released her belt and button on her pants. "No buts. Donna is gone. No one will know."

He crouched down as he took her pants to the floor. He placed a long, tender kiss over her mons and inhaled.

Her stomach clenched.

"Baby, I need hours with you to make up for being without you."

She moaned. His hand cupped each ankle as she stepped of her pants.

She wove her fingers through his hair as he stroked her thighs up and down. "Take off your bra, Lily."

She licked her lips; there was no turning back, and despite herself, she did as he commanded.

He rose and quickly took both needy breasts in his hand. He sucked a pointed nipple into his mouth. She cried out.

Brandon loved all the sounds of ecstasy that flew out of Lily's mouth. He loved his hands and his mouth on her naked body. He laved on her other breast, and her back bowed, pushing into him.

74

Her hands reached for his stomach, exploring, and smoothing down his hard length.

"Undo my pants. See how desperate I am for you."

Her delicate fingers trembled slightly as she unfastened his belt and pants, and sent them to the floor. She slid beneath his briefs' waistband, wrapping one hand around him.

As she pumped her fist slowly, he grazed his hands down the sides of her feminine body and slid her panties aside. He wasted no time letting his fingers explore her warm, swollen pussy.

"So wet, Lily." He easily plunged two fingers inside her, relishing her moans. He continued to pump and twist, watching the flush brighten in her cheeks. She was close already.

"You are so beautiful, Lily." She opened her eyes.

"Brandon, no one's ever made me feel this way."

He couldn't wait another minute, he had to be inside her.

He hooked his fingers in her panties and dragged them to the floor. Then he hoisted her onto the edge of the desk and stepped between her legs. Her legs wrapped around his waist, and aligning his cock he drove into her hot channel.

They both moaned. He would never grow tired of this; the feeling of connecting with Lily in this way was beyond anything he could fathom.

He pumped more, hearing only their panting breaths and the slip-slide of their joining.

"Brandon," she breathed.

"Lie back."

She glanced over her shoulder. "But the papers."

"They don't matter. Lie back."

As she did, he smoothed a finger over her hard little numb and her hips convulsed.

She gripped the desk, her head barely able to rest on the top, and pumped her hips in time with his. In a few short moments, her muscles began pulling and squeezing him as her climax came to full speed.

She groaned and bowed her back off the desk. *Stunning.*

He quickly pulled out and came on her stomach. He wasn't nearly satisfied.

He bent down before her, holding onto her thighs as he made love to her pussy with his mouth. She shrieked, no doubt still sensitive from her orgasm.

He lifted her legs onto his shoulders when she pumped her hips against his mouth. He licked her clit and poked inside her repeatedly. She tasted of ambrosia.

He pressed harder on her clit, and her hands gripped the hair on his head as another climax flew to the surface.

She stifled a scream.

When the tremors mostly subsided, he rose and gently pushed his erect cock back where it belonged. Inside the love of his life.

He leaned over, skin to skin, pumping more slowly this time. "You taste exactly as you did that very first night, love. I'll never forget that first night in Rome."

He lowered to her incredibly sensual mouth.

Her arms and legs wrapped around him, cocooning him. They moved as one. He wove his fingers through her hair, protecting her head from his hard desk, while his tongue danced with hers.

His balls grew heavy, and he didn't know how much longer he could last. But fuck, he didn't want it to end.

As if hearing his thoughts, she said, "Brandon, don't hold back. We have tonight." Her lips curled into that precious smile of hers.

She was right. He had more work to do, but they would be together tonight, and more nights after that.

He drew back and slammed into her. She moaned, and in no time his seed spurted inside her, releasing more tension from the last two weeks without her.

"Oh wow," she panted.

He breathed into her shoulder and chuckled. "Hang on. I'll get a towel."

He slowly withdrew, and with one holding his pants, he dampened two towels at the sink. He gingerly wiped her sex, then her belly.

"Miss Bennett, you are one fine woman. And the best thing that has happened to my desk, ever."

She giggled. "We broke a rule," she said with a shy smile.

"And it was well worth it."

Properly clean, she stood to redress as he put himself back together. "Um, so why did I get a weird feeling from Donna earlier?"

He looked up from buttoning his shirt. "Well, she knows about us, so I suspect she made an excuse to leave us alone." He'd need to remember to give that woman a raise.

Lily gasped and her eyes rounded as big as saucers. "She knows?"

He stepped closer, taking her hands. "It's okay. She won't say a word. She's very loyal to me. She's been with me for years. And she likes you."

She licked her lips, only mildly relaxed.

"Trust me. It's okay."

Looking down, she zipped her pants closed. "If you say so. I really don't want people thinking I got this job because of our relationship."

"I understand. She'll be very discreet. Have you noticed the phone didn't ring once?" He gave her a full-on smile, and her cheeks reddened with embarrassment.

"Great. She knew what we were doing in here."

He couldn't help but chuckle. Their relationship may be under wraps for now. But if Brandon had his way, it wouldn't be for long.

Chapter 11

AT BRANDON'S REQUEST—command, really—
she took a cab to his condo for Andrew to let her in.
She wanted to get back to her place, but it didn't feel
much like home yet, so what was the difference,
really?

As the door opened, several vases of Brandon's
signature red roses sat strategically around his condo.
Beautiful. His lavish attention made her feel like a
queen.

She quickly got settled and strode to the kitchen
for a glass of wine, when a black velvet box caught
her eye. A tented note card sat behind it: *Welcome
home, my love. Brandon.*

Oh my. He was *really* going to spoil her.

No wonder he wanted her there.

She slipped off the ribbon and opened the tiny
square box. Glimmering back at her were a pair of
diamond stud earrings.

Gees! They must be a carat each!

Box in hand, she went to the bathroom mirror and slipped off the simple hoops she wore, replacing them with her new gift.

Wow! These were too much, but they looked so amazing on. If she was living a dream, she never wanted to wake up.

Maybe she could give Brandon an extra special "thank you" later. She smiled at that thought.

For the next few hours, she got caught up on email, including her parents and Court, cleaned all her laundry except what she'd take to the dry cleaners, and changed into jeans and a t-shirt. She munched on some carrot sticks when Brandon texted.

Meeting running over. Help yourself to the dinner the cook left, I'll see you soon. Miss you! B

She glanced at the time—seven-thirty. No wonder she was hungry. She went to the fridge and began warming the beef stew the cook made earlier.

She forced her focus on the dinner, because she couldn't let her disappointment bring her down. *Lil, he's a busy man. You knew this going in.*

She smiled, glad she'd seen him earlier in his office. Her face warmed at the memory. Brandon was a fantastic lover. And his natural draw to adventure in that area brought out her adventurous side. Her nature had always been more reserved. Well, that disappeared when he'd walked through her hotel room door in Rome months ago.

Where would they be if that hadn't happened?

With dinner finished, she took her wine and retreated to the bathtub. She could soak for a while as she waited for Brandon.

By ten o'clock, she slipped on one of his t-shirts, pulled out a book to read, and settled into bed. It must be very important for Brandon to be so late—he'd never come home this late before.

When his sister, Katie, and his head of manufacturing, Randy showed up at his office as he was packing up for the night, he knew something was wrong. The rock in his gut confirmed it.

"Hey, Brandon," Katie started, "got a moment?"

He knew "a moment" would not be "a moment". *Damn!*

"Sure, shall we sit?" He directed them to his conference table. "So what's going on?"

Katie laid down an unfolded sheet of paper and spun it around toward Brandon. A quick glance showed it was an inquiry from the FDA, Food and Drug Administration. *What?*

He leveled a look at Katie. "What is this?"

"First, we were sorta expecting this. And second it's just an inquiry."

"Sort of expecting this?" His voice rose. "What does that mean?" He would not lose his shit unless absolutely necessary.

Randy chimed in. "We got some feedback from a hospital chain in California. They are reporting issues with our ECG monitor."

"The regulations for this equipment are different in California—"

"How so?" he interrupted his sister.

"They have a more specific protocol for how the electrodes can be placed on the body."

Brandon couldn't help himself, he rolled his eyes. This wasn't the first time he saw government stand in the way of good medicine.

"So the hospital training addressed this protocol, but inadvertently when an order went out it included the standard documentation we send to the other forty-nine states," Randy said.

Katie raised her hand, knowing how Brandon hated mistakes. "We quickly alerted them and sent the proper documentation."

"Can I see the two pieces of documentation?" he asked.

"Sure," Randy punched out a text to someone. "It should be here shortly."

Brandon ran a hand through his hair. "I hate scrutiny from the FDA, folks."

"I know. And normally, this would be a non-issue, except this particular hospital chain has a policy to send a letter when patient care is affected."

"Christ." Brandon felt the heat rise from his chest to his neck.

For the next several hours, they sat and reviewed the two sets of documentation Laurel had to ship. They reviewed the process as the ECG went down the manufacturing line. Then they got the California sales rep on the phone to review the letter. Katie took notes to formulate a response to the FDA, and one of his corporate lawyers showed up an hour ago to read it and take it back for finalizing.

Fuck! He couldn't leave the office with this potential red-flag hanging over their heads. He'd texted Lily, but that didn't assuage the knot in his gut about leaving her alone tonight.

Finally at a little after ten, they all headed home and agreed to meet the next afternoon.

He was beat—physically and emotionally drained. He walked into the quiet condo, seeing only a single light on in the kitchen, and no sign of Lily.

He dropped his case, jacket, and tie on the chair, and went in search of his woman. He crossed the bedroom threshold and saw her lying with a book still in her hand, asleep in his bed. She wore her new earrings and one of his white t-shirts, her face without a stitch of makeup and she looked like an angel.

His heart ached and warmed at the same time.

This was her first night back, and he'd been stuck in the office. Sometimes life sucked.

He walked to her, carefully slipping the book out of her hand, and placed a kiss on her forehead before switching off the bedside lamp.

This should have been their night together. Well, he would find a way to make it up to her.

Chapter 12

LILY AWOKE TO a soft stroking down the bridge of her nose. It was so subtle, she wasn't sure it was real. When she caught the scent of roses, she knew it was no dream. She pried her eyes open to see Brandon smiling down on her, red rose in hand.

"Good morning, beautiful."

"Good morning." She couldn't help but smile back at him.

Dressed in a dark gray suit with a red silk tie, he looked handsome and powerful, and oh so yummy. *What is it about a man in a suit?*

"Lily, I'm sorry about last night. We got a letter from the FDA, and I couldn't let it rest."

"Oh no." She lifted up on her elbow.

"It'll be okay, but I have to leave early this morning."

She could see that, and tried hard not to let her disappointment show. "Okay."

"I want to go out Saturday night. Whatever you want—dinner, dancing, a movie. I know work has been busier lately for me. It should calm down soon."

"I'd like that." Although truthfully, she didn't need all the fanfare. She was a simple girl. They could stay in and eat a casual dinner, talk, and watch a movie on TV. They hadn't seen each other in two weeks.

"Oh, and I need to tell you. My good friend, Courtney, from California is coming to visit in a few weeks."

"That's great. So you both will stay at your place, right? No boys allowed?"

She chuckled. This was a man who had sisters. "Yes, sorry baby. No boys allowed."

"Damn. Okay, and you have another trip to Rome, right?"

"I do." In eight days, if her memory served. However, that trip only required her to stay for a week.

"So, let's talk more about it this weekend." He tilted forward to kiss her sweetly. "Have a great day, sexy."

She smiled. "You too."

She took one last sniff of the rose and stuck it in the vase with the others. *How does he get roses delivered so early in the morning?*

Lily strolled to the kitchen, and after fixing her coffee, she sidled onto a barstool to check her personal email and scope out a few things to do while Court was in town. So many great places to eat, shop, clubs to hit.

Oh, this is gonna be so much fun.

Because of the seven-hour time difference with Rome, she decided to check her work email. Lily received the occasional message from the transition team in Italy.

Thankfully, her inbox wasn't packed. She read a reminder about a meeting later on the fifth floor, and another later in the week on eight. Just once she wished they'd have a meeting on twenty. She smiled as she continuing thumbing through. She'd *love* to run into Brandon. See his smile. See him in his hot, sexy command-mode. Know they had a hidden secret that no one but Donna and his sisters knew about. She sighed.

An email from Emma popped up. She knew Lily was returning to Rome soon and wanted to do dinner out some night during the week.

Wow. What a lovely gesture. She replied immediately with a resounding yes. She really liked Emma. Best she could tell, they were both about the same age and had similar interests. Maybe Emma could even come to the States sometime. Lily could show her around. Maybe they'd run into a real-life cowboy. She giggled at herself. They'd definitely need to find the best bacon cheeseburger in town.

But enough of that, she had to shower and get ready for work. Plus, since she was going to Rome, she could stand to work out an extra time or two this week, so she'd need to grab her workout clothes.

Chapter 13

LILY'S PHONE RANG around eight fifteen Friday morning. She'd just come out of the bathroom. Trying not to wake Courtney, she dashed out of the bedroom. "Good morning."

"Good morning, sexy. How are you?"

She smiled every time Brandon called her sexy. She loved it. "I'm good."

"Not hungover?"

"Nope. We were good last night. Just dinner and a movie. Now tonight could be a different story," she giggled.

"Oh? Going clubbing?"

"Well, the plan is to go shopping. Later dinner, and then Court and I are going to Glass. I heard good things about it. And we both like to dance, so it should be fun."

"Okay. I'll have Gerry take you around tonight. What time should he be there?"

"What? You don't have to do that."

"Sure. Especially if you want to drink, then you don't have to worry."

"Thanks, Brandon. How about seven-thirty?"

"Done. So, now that you're up, go to the door."

"What?"

"Go to your door."

What is he up to? She hesitated, but with her phone in one hand, she opened the door with the other.

Her face relaxed when she saw Brandon standing before her, smiling as he leaned against the wall outside her apartment.

"Hello, gorgeous."

"Hello, handsome."

"I wanted to bring you a little something."

Her brows lifted. "Really? I'm starting to get the impression you like surprising me."

He grinned and pulled a little black box from his jacket pocket.

Gees! She knew something good was coming.

He lifted the lid and in the box sat a beautiful pair of silver hoop earrings with emerald gemstones set in a channel.

Gasping, she said, "Emeralds. My birthstone."

"I know."

She reached for them and cupped the box. *So thoughtful.* "Oh, Brandon. They're beautiful. Thank you." She glanced up at him through her eyelashes.

He stepped forward, snaked an arm around her waist, and pulled her closer.

She was in flannel boxers and a t-shirt, but couldn't care less if someone saw her. She circled her arms around his neck, and from her tiptoes, she crashed her lips to his. He sank his tongue into her

88

mouth—caressing and tangling. One of his hands grazed down her hip and gripped her bottom, pulling her into him. Heat began to build in her nether parts, and she knew she had to stop.

He backed off the kiss and rested his lips on her forehead. "I love having you in my arms, Lily. But we can't get carried away. You have company, and I have work."

She smiled as she inhaled the exquisite cologne he wore. "Yes."

He stepped back, and smiled down at her. "Gerry will be here at seven-thirty. Have fun tonight." And with one last peck on her lips, he jogged to the car in the parking lot.

How the hell did she get so lucky?

***

"These are the best jeans in the world," Courtney called from Lily's bathroom.

"Come out. Let me see."

Court stepped out into the bedroom wearing her new slim-fitting blue jeans that taper at the bottom, strappy heels, and a sparkling silver top.

"Dang. You look good."

"Thanks," her eyes widened, "so do you."

Sometimes, Lily felt like she and Courtney were polar opposites. Court was thin and statuesque with long, shiny brown hair and big brown eyes. Lily had shoulder-length wavy hair, blue eyes, and definitely more curves.

Lily was flattered by Brandon's appreciation of her curves, the curves she felt self-conscience about. Ironically, she was losing a few pounds. Likely because of all the sex. Brandon couldn't seem to get enough of her. Not that she was complaining.

She stood to do a final check in the mirror. Everything looked and felt good, including her new jeans.

"Gerry should be out there. Ready?"

"Yup." Court grabbed her clutch from the chair and the ladies headed outside to their waiting chariot.

Brandon walked into the club, the music pulsing and people everywhere. Mostly standing and drinking, trying to talk over the loud music.

He had to give it to the owners, they were sitting on a goldmine. He meandered, searching for Lily and Courtney through the dimly lit space, when Lily's dancing body caught his attention. Both women were out on the dancefloor, dancing to some song with a strong beat.

Brandon's sight locked on Lily and his cock flexed.

He hung back in the shadows and watched.

Holy fuck!

His woman moved easily and fluidly to the beat. When she stretched her arms overhead, her breasts enticed him.

And apparently, someone else as well.

Two guys joined the dancing duo, one coming up behind Lily, moving as she moved. She didn't seem to care either way. Heat rose to Brandon's face. He was ready to fly to the dancefloor and knock the punk on his ass. Instead he stayed rooted. This was Lily's night out with her best friend. She didn't need some jealous boyfriend crashing it and ruining her good time.

She spun around and continued her gyrations. Brandon's eyes glued to her beautifully rounded ass in her tight, dark denim jeans. He didn't recognize them. Perhaps she'd bought them when they'd gone shopping. She wore a body-conscious top and the hoop earrings he'd given her earlier.

Even with some guy trying to put the moves on his girlfriend, Brandon was absolutely mesmerized watching her dance. She smiled and laughed almost the whole time. And when the guy held onto her hips, Brandon didn't flinch. Despite himself, his cock only grew.

She looked fucking amazing out there.

He watched them for another two songs when the girls waved goodbye to their dance partners, and headed to a tiny round table at the other end of the club.

He should go. Really, he should. He'd simply wanted to pop in, maybe say hello, and head home for a late dinner and a tall beer.

So why did he text her?

Lily panted on the dancefloor, breaking a little sweat. It felt good to let loose with Court, really let her hair down and have some fun. As she and Court made their way back to the table, she flagged down their waitress and ordered two cherry bomb shots with beer chasers.

"Girl, you are lettin' it all hang out tonight," Courtney said, angling back in her chair, an eyebrow lifted.

She shrugged a shoulder. "Eh. I figure one, I can sleep in tomorrow. And two, Brandon gave us the limo tonight, so neither one of us has to drive."

"You know it, sister."

91

The drinks arrived a minute later, which was perfect. She was parched.

"Here's to my bestie and her filthy rich boyfriend," Court said as she raised her shot.

Lily chuckled. "Cheers."

And simultaneously they downed their shots. Lily reached for her beer and took a swig. She licked her lips. "Awesome."

She felt her phone buzz in the mini-purse slung across her body. The corners of her lips lifted.

"What is it?" Court asked.

"A text from Brandon."

She opened and read it.

Having fun?

"He wants to know if we're having a good time."

"Hell, yes."

She replied.

We are. What are you doing?

She stared at her screen for his response.

Waiting on you. I'm in the back.

She gasped.

"What?" Court's eyes widened.

She looked up at her friend. "Brandon's here. He wants to see me."

"Holy crap. He's here. He's been watching us." Courtney's head darted left and right, searching. Then an insane grin crossed her face. "Well, go see what he wants."

"Will you be alright?"

"Yes, of course. Go. Go." She pushed gently on Lily's shoulder.

"Okay, I'll be right back."

Lily was intrigued. Her heart-rate ratcheted up. She wend through the crowd toward the back of the club. Down a hall, she passed the restrooms, a door marked "office", and just one other door, which was closed. *Where is he?*

Suddenly, she felt an arm hook around her waist and pull her backward.

A little yelp escaped.

"Ssh," Brandon whispered in her ear.

"Where are we?" she whispered.

"A linen closet."

She couldn't see much of anything.

"What are you doing here?"

He didn't answer her question. Instead he pivoted her to a shelving unit and placed her hands on an upper shelf. Then his hands roamed down her arms, the sides of her torso, and over her hips and ass.

"I dropped in to say hi, and saw you dancing," his hands skimmed over her ass and circled her thighs, "in these very tight jeans."

Her breathing came heavier as Brandon caressed her. "Um, yes. They're new."

"I like them." He glazed a hand across her front, moving lower, over her sex.

"Oh," she breathed. Unknowingly, she spread her stance.

Brandon didn't let up. His hands climbed under her shirt to her breasts, and he eased her bra down over her breasts. He toyed with her nipples. "You looked like you were having a lot of fun."

She pushed her chest into his hands and dropped her head on his shoulder. "Brandon," she moaned. Lust flooded her veins.

"Yes, baby. Did you have fun dancing? Maybe dancing with that guy? Was that fun?"

She couldn't process the words as he tormented her this way. He wasn't mad, was he?

He pushed his rock-hard erection into the crevice of her ass. "I wanted to be that guy, pressing up behind you as you moved that sweet ass."

She moaned.

He stroked his fingers over her sex. "I can feel the heat from your delicious pussy coming through these jeans."

"Brandon, please," she pleaded. She needed more. This man could turn her on with his gentle touch and soft words. She craved him, her body craved him.

He leaned close, licked the shell of her ear, and asked, "Do you want my cock inside you, baby? Do you need to come?"

"Yes. Yes, Brandon. Please."

He unfastened her jeans. "We'll have to be quick, so you can get back to Courtney."

He crouched down, pulling against the fabric, and slipped off one heel, then her pant leg. His lips planted several kisses on her bare ass.

Her wet pussy chilled in the exposed air.

She heard Brandon work his pants zipper. "Lily, this ass is mine." His fingers slid through the tender flesh between her legs.

She arched her back giving him access.

"And I am so glad you gave it to me." He slowly pushed into her.

A throaty groan slipped passed her lips.

"You feel amazing. I'll fuck you fast," his hands went back to her breasts as he pumped into her, "and after Courtney leaves, I'll make love to you for as long as you want."

"Yes," she breathed.

She could feel her climax building already. Brandon hadn't even stimulated her clit. He only twisted and tugged her nipples as he thrusted.

Her muscles clenched around his cock, and he growled in her ear. The orgasm was so fast and intense, the waves of lust raced through her body electrifying her.

Brandon pumped harder and released his orgasm with a groan.

He gently pulled out, and quickly placed a towel in her hand. She wiped away what she could and put her clothes back on.

She looked at him now, the first time since that morning, and smiled.

"Baby, that was amazing." He cradled her face in his hands and fastened his mouth to hers. "Now, go out there and have fun. You know where to find me if you need me."

He kissed her deeply as she clung to him, loving the feel of his strong arms around her and his passionate lips on her.

He broke the kiss. "Okay. Thanks for stopping by." She giggled, the effects of the alcohol setting in.

"Okay, let's go." He spun her toward the door and swatted her ass.

She squealed and slowly opened the door to make sure no one would notice them. "The coast is clear."

With a hand on her low back, he guided her to their table just as a waitress delivered fresh drinks.

Brandon quickly retrieved his money clip from his front pocket, pulled out two one-hundred dollar bills, and set them on the waitress's tray. "This should cover the drinks, the rest is yours."

Her eyes lit up. "Thank you, sir."

"Thanks, Brandon," Courtney said with an exuberant smile on her face.

"You're welcome. Thanks for letting me steal Lily for a minute." Then he reached for Courtney's hand and kissed the back. She practically swooned.

He gave Lily the same treatment, and added a wink. "You ladies have fun tonight."

"Oh, we will." They replied in unison, and Brandon chuckled before he headed for the front door.

"Oh my God, Lily. He is the best." Courtney spun in her seat to face her. "What happened?" Her voice dipped conspiratorially.

"What do you think happened?"

After a brief pause, she said, "I think he found some dark corner and fucked you until you came."

Lily's face grew hot, but she smiled. "That's exactly what happened."

"Oh, you lucky bitch. Does Brandon have a brother?"

They both laughed, and took a large swig of beer before heading back to the dancefloor.

Chapter 14

THE AUTUMN FLEW by faster than Brandon could ever remember. Maybe this year felt different because he had a reason to want time to slow down—Lily.

Work could be another reason. Business was good, but that meant more work for everyone including himself. Which reminded him . . .

He picked up his desk phone. "Donna, would you set a meeting next week with all the department heads, separate meetings if necessary? Tell them I want to review year-end bonuses. Make sure everything's in line."

"Yes, sir."

"Thank you."

Turning his attention back to his computer screen, he reviewed his calendar for the day. It would be a busy one.

He looked forward to the next day when Lily returned from her third trip to Rome. He smirked recalling their conversation when she left. He'd promised her he wouldn't beckon her to his office. Fair enough, but he'd do his damnedest to get away from the office early so he could meet her at home.

Until then, he had several things on his list to tackle.

Brandon picked up the phone to speak to his VP of Information Technology.

"Ken, I was reading in the Journal yesterday about a cyber attack at Bellmont. How are we looking on our end? Have we been affected?"

"Well, I heard about that."

"Yeah?" Ken was never one to simply spit it out.

"Brandon, there are always potential problems. Whether it's with wireless networks, cybersecurity, and even software upgrades."

He had to swallow back a chuckle. Ken was constantly "glass half-empty". But Ken sought out areas that were weak, areas that could cause future problems. Most importantly, Ken always gave him the truth and that's what Brandon paid him for.

"I understand that."

"I'm going to run some tests, double-check firewalls, etcetera, but from our perspective, we are completely unaffected."

"Ken, I appreciate it. I know you've got it under control. Just checking in to make sure you didn't need anything from me."

"No, boss. We're good."

Good to know. Attacks against companies' data—secret or not—seemed to be on the rise. Thankfully so did the technology to combat it.

Just as he hung up the phone, Donna rapped on the door jamb. "Leena is on the phone for you."

"Okay, put her through."

He held the phone to his ear. "Sis, you know you can call me on my cell."

"I know, I know. But I don't what to bug you if you're busy."

"It's okay. What's going on?"

"Two things. One, I have an update on improvements at the Worthington plant. But first, let's talk about Katie's wedding."

"Oh, here we go."

They laughed, but his little sister always had his back, whether it was tossing him a water bottle before baseball practice or telling him when his fly was down. She reminded him to make hotel reservations, if they chose to stay, and most importantly, that he'd need to buy a gift.

"Can't I just write a check?"

"Nooo. That's tacky."

"Alright. I'll take Lily shopping with me this weekend."

"Perfect. Speaking of which, how are things going with you two?"

"Good. She's in Rome, but comes home tomorrow."

"Good, huh?"

"You don't believe me?" He pulled the Worthington plant folder from his file drawer.

"I just want to make sure. This is your first *real* relationship. Relationships require a lot of care and attention. You know that, right?"

He bit back a sigh. "I do."

"And that means not just pulling out your wallet. Lily needs to feel special, not bought."

"Ouch!"

Brandon knew his sister wanted to help him, and he hated to admit it, but she might have a point. His memory took him back to the shopping trip at Bachendorf's.

"That means work cannot always come first." Leena might know a thing or two. She and Bekah have been together for over five years.

"I'm running a company here—"

"With very competent people working for you. You don't have to be responsible for everything. The weight of the company doesn't rest on your shoulders."

But it does, at least in the eyes of investors.

"Bran, don't blow it with Lily. I know how you can be. And you don't always have to be so available."

"Alright, I hear you. And this is an awfully big conversation to be having this early in the morning."

"Fine. Change of subject."

Leena went on to give him a progress report of some changes made to one of their manufacturing facilities outside of Miami. He listened, but felt anxious to wrap the conversation. When she dropped off, Leena's words replayed in his head.

Was he showering Lily with gifts to make up for not being around?

He wanted her to have nice things. He would buy her anything she wanted. *Girls like bling, right?*

His cheeks pillowed when he exhaled.

Admittedly, he didn't have much experience with romantic relationships. Brandon put work before dating.

What can I do?

He knew things were sometimes strained between him and Lily.

He saw the sadness in her eyes, more than once, when he had to work after dinner. He could hear the disappointment in her voice sometimes over the phone when he had to work late in the office. He was sure she tried to hide it, but Brandon knew his girl.

He didn't like working so many hours, but it came with the job. And truly, a lot of this was end-of-year stuff. Things would settle down after the first of the year. He was confident of it.

Chapter 15

BRANDON SAT NEXT to Lily, on the second row of the church pew. His fingers interlaced with hers, and from the corner of her eye she saw him watch the ceremony.

Katie and Tim kept the ceremony simple. The old church was the same church Tim's parents got married in. It was beautifully decorated with bouquets of flowers and lit candles. Lily estimated a hundred people were in attendance with six attendees in the wedding party. Understated elegance were the words that came to mind.

She could see getting married in an old stone church like that.

After the ceremony and the requisite photos taken, Brandon escorted her to the hotel ballroom. She felt like she was walking through a fairytale: the gown, the chariot, and her handsome prince. Giddiness filled her from head to toe.

When dinner finished, the band played and the emcee announced the bride and groom for their first dance. Lily listened to the vocalist sing about how people fall in love in mysterious ways, and she sighed. How true were those words?

Brandon rose and extended his hand to her, smiling. "Would you like to dance?"

She placed her hand in his and let him lead her to the dance floor. They danced arm in arm, and Lily rested her cheek against his chest. Could she ask for a more perfect night?

"Did I tell you how beautiful you look tonight?"

She grinned and nodded. "You did, thank you. And thank you for these lovely earrings. You are spoiling me."

"That's good."

"The ceremony was beautiful."

"It was," Brandon replied with a smile as he spun her on the dance floor.

"Tim and Katie look very happy together." And watching them exchange vows and their first kiss had Lily thinking—fantasizing, really—what it would be like to marry Brandon. She had tried to push the thought away, but she dared herself to think that it *might* be possible.

"They do look happy." Brandon turned his head toward the happy couple in the middle of the dance floor. "Tim adores her. They'll be good for each other."

Daniel Morgan approached them. "Son, mind if I cut in?"

What a handsome man Brandon's father was, just a bit shorter than Brandon with a smattering of gray at the temples and sideburns.

"I don't mind if Lily doesn't mind," he grinned.

"I'd love to."

Brandon pecked her on the cheek. "I'll head to the restroom. Back in a few," he whispered in her ear.

She nodded. She'd met Daniel at the rehearsal dinner the previous night, but hadn't had much of an opportunity to talk with him or Brandon's mother.

"So, Brandon tells me you two met on a plane ride over to Rome and now you work for Laurel."

She smiled. "Yes. You've created a wonderful company, Mr. Morgan."

"Daniel, please. I am proud of Laurel, but immensely proud of Brandon and his sisters for stepping up when I couldn't lead anymore."

"You should be."

"I am fortunate that they all played a part in the success of the company, and were willing to take over." The glint in his eyes turned more thoughtful. "I'm glad he found someone like you, Lily. I worried that he was working too hard for his own good, but my son seems very happy right now."

"Thank you." Her cheeks warmed under his compliments.

They danced to the five-piece band and chatted some more. Pride beamed from Daniel's face when he spoke of his children. Chatting with him made Lily think about Brandon as a father.

Does he even want children?

Daniel led her back to the table after the song ended. "Thank you for the dance, Lily. I'm off to find my wife."

Sandra was a lovely, elegant woman who seemed equally content chatting at high-society functions or feeding horses and chickens on a farm.

She smiled and nodded.

Lily took a long sip of water and combed the ballroom. She didn't see Brandon anywhere.

Surely, he had to be back from the restroom? Lily drummed her fingers against the table. Several long minutes passed and she grew concerned. She twisted the napkin in her lap as she continued to survey the room.

She rose from her chair and strolled to Leena and her girlfriend, Bekah, who were standing at the bar, refreshing their drinks.

"Have either of you seen Brandon?"

Their gazes traveled the room as a collective. "No, I haven't," Leena replied as she narrowed her eyes.

"Okay. Thanks. I'm sure he's around here somewhere." She wondered if he'd taken a work call. Hadn't they agreed to put work away for the day?

Lily's nerves were on edge. She wasn't used to being alone at a big affair, such as this.

Heading toward the bathrooms to see if he was okay, she crossed the ballroom and turned down a short hall to find the closest men's room. She passed an elderly woman, who'd smiled at her. As she neared the corner of the hallway, she heard Brandon's voice. Then it went quiet. Was he on the phone?

She rounded the turn just in time to see his ex-girlfriend, Rachel, with her arms around Brandon—his back against the wall, she leaning in, kissing him.

Lily made a half-step back and her hand flew over her mouth, covering her gasp. *Oh God!*

She spun around and willed her feet to carry her back to the table. Her poor little heart raced in her chest, hammering away like it had just run a marathon. Her stomach churned as she eased into her seat. God, she couldn't think, couldn't focus. What had she just witnessed?

Brandon passed through the bathroom door into the hall and was instantly greeted by Rachel, his ex-girlfriend, whose boyfriend was good friends with Tim. Her perfume overpowered the air around her.

"Hello, Brandon."

"Hello, Rachel."

This woman had a lot of natural, beautiful assets, like her blonde hair, thin physique, and peaches and cream complexion. The allowance from her trust allowed her to enhance any of those features she wished. Including her false eyelashes that fluttered as she smiled.

"I thought I'd find you." She flipped her long hair behind her shoulder. "So are you having fun with your precious little date?"

He didn't much appreciate Rachel's tone, but now was not the time or place to get into it with her.

"Oh, I mean no offence. She's certainly the chubbiest girl you've ever dated."

"You're mistaken if you think your opinion matters to me. Goodbye, Rachel."

As he tried to sidle by, her arms went up over his shoulders, pinning him to the wall. Then she eased forward, planting her lips over his.

He quickly gripped her shoulders, forcing Rachel back. "What's gotten into you?"

"You. I want you *in* to me," she said with a repulsive grin on her face.

"Rachel, what about Mike? Aren't you seeing him? Why the hell are you coming on to me?"

"Mike will understand. You and I have always been good together."

"No, we haven't," he said with a heavy sigh. "And Lily *will not* understand. I'm in a committed relationship, in case you haven't noticed."

"I *have* noticed. I didn't think you had it in you," she said as she stroked a fingernail slowly down his chest.

Brandon grabbed Rachel's finger and brought it to the side of her body. "I do have it in me. In fact, I've never been happier." His voice dropped. "I suggest you stop prowling and stay true to Mike. He's a good guy. Otherwise, break it off."

He pushed passed her to make his way back to the ballroom and his beautiful date.

The object of his thoughts sat at their table, looking gorgeous as ever in her pink dress and dangling silver earrings. The emcee announced that Katie and Tim should join him up front to cut the cake.

Brandon took his seat next to Lily who didn't seem to notice his return. Before he could say anything, Rachel approached.

"Would you two like some cake? I'll get you a slice." She gave a sickly-sweet smile, spun around, and left.

He had no interest in anything from Rachel— their last interaction left a foul taste in his mouth. He turned to speak with Lily who was looking up were Rachel had just stood. Her skin was pale.

He laid a hand on her forearm. "Lily, are you alright?" She glanced his way, a look in her eyes he'd never seen before, and then stared back at her hands.

He reached below the table and gripped her fingers. He leaned close, as the table began filling up with guests looking to eat their cake. "Lily, what's wrong?"

She finally looked at him, not saying a word. She lifted his white napkin off the table, gently blotted his lips, and set the napkin on the table. He wouldn't have given it much thought, but his eyes tracked her hand and looked at the napkin. There, smeared on the white fabric, a hint of Rachel's red lipstick.

Shit! His head shot up and he saw Lily blink several times before hanging her head again.

"Wait here."

This would not do. His blood pressure ratcheted up a hundred points as he realized that Lily had seen Rachel's little escapade. Brandon had to fix this, but not here. He found his parents and his sisters to say goodbye.

"Katie," he leaned down to kiss her cheek, "you look beautiful—congratulations. Lily isn't feeling well, so I'm taking her to the room. I'm sure we'll see you tomorrow at brunch."

His sister pulled her brows together. "Yes, of course. Tell her I hope she feels better."

He returned to Lily and took her hand. "Let's go."

She looked up at him and rose slowly. He slid her chair back, and pulled her away from the disastrous ending to a beautiful event.

She was quiet. Too quiet. And his gut felt like lead for the pain she was feeling. Witnessing that stunt Rachel pulled, in addition to not having as much alone-time together, must be salt on an open wound.

He led her into their room, and immediately blasted the hot water in the bathroom sink.

"What are you doing?" she finally spoke, watching his reflection in the mirror.

He slipped off his jacket, and laid it and his bowtie on the vanity countertop. He rolled up his sleeves and grabbed the soap. "I'm getting any residue of that woman off me."

She stood there, stock-still, while he scrubbed his face.

"You're going to make your skin raw."

Maybe she was right, but this was for Lily's benefit as much as his. He stopped and towel-dried his face.

He met her eyes, before she glanced away.

He reached for her chin to force her to meet his gaze. "She's an ex-girlfriend."

"I know that." She tried to look away, but he didn't let her.

"What you don't know is that *she* kissed *me*. Did you see anything after she kissed me?"

Lily shook her head.

"I pushed her away. I told her I was with you. That I wasn't interested."

Her eyebrows lifted slightly. "You did?"

He stepped closer and cupped his hands around her jaw. Her blue eyes shimmered with unshed tears. "I did. Lily, I'm sorry you saw Rachel's antics."

A tear chased down her cheek. "I was in shock, I think. I didn't handle this very well." She waved her hand absently.

He leaned forward to place a little kiss on precious lips. "Don't doubt for a moment how I feel about you, sweetheart."

She lowered her eyes and shrugged a shoulder. "I know. I'm sorry."

She was sorry. He pulled her close, wrapping his arms around her warm body. He would give anything to never see that wounded expression on her face again.

He kissed her forehead. "How about we get out of these clothes, order s'mores from room service, and cuddle in front of a movie?"

She inclined her head and grinned. "You can do that?"

He tipped his head. "Order a movie?"

"No, silly. Order s'mores."

He pecked her with one last kiss and headed into the bedroom. "Sure. Anything for a price."

She grabbed the closest pillow she could find and chucked it at him. He only let out a mocking laugh when it struck his back.

They sat comfortably, watching the popular comedic movie for several minutes when Lily straightened from her reclined position and looked at him. "Brandon, can you tell me about Rachel?"

"Okay." He picked up the remote to pause the movie. "We dated for a while last year. I guess you could say she was the closest thing I had to a girlfriend in my adult life."

"So, what happened?"

He shrugged a shoulder. "We fought more with each passing day."

"Fought because you weren't paying much attention to her?"

He curved his lips into a rueful smile. "You are very perceptive. That's exactly it. I worked too much for us to sustain a relationship."

She nodded. "And do you miss her?"

He shook his head. "Not even a little bit. If you had seen everything that happened in the hall, you would know." He took her hands, stroking his thumbs over her knuckles. "Lily, know that I don't love her. I love you. I want to be with you."

Her smile lit up the room. "I love you, too. And I'm very sorry about ending our evening the way we did. I hope Katie isn't mad at me."

"She's fine. We'll see her at brunch tomorrow. Now, can we finish our movie? Afterward, I'd like to take you to that enormous bed and show you just what you mean to me."

She grinned and a beautiful blush crept over her cheeks.

He tucked her back into his side as they relaxed, truly relaxed, if only for a short time.

He had exactly what he wanted with Lily. What he'd had with Rachel never had the makings for long-term. Lily and he were happy, and nothing would change that.

Chapter 16

SHE WAS A genius. *Oh my God, it's perfect.*

Lily stared out into space, running the whole present through her head. *Oh, he will love it.*

She had the answer to the question plaguing her for some time now—what to get Brandon for Christmas? A man who had everything.

A massage.

She owed him something special, especially after Katie's wedding and how she'd reacted to the Rachel fiasco. Lily wanted to rip the woman's face off. It may have taken some time to accept it, but she belonged to Brandon and Brandon belonged to her. Rachel had no business coming on to her man.

Brandon handled the incident with grace, and didn't berate her for how she'd flipped out. At that moment—witnessing him and Rachel kissing—it had been like the floor opened up and she'd gone free-falling down, completely lost without Brandon. He remained a complete gentleman, and thought of nothing but her and how she felt. He deserved something wonderful.

Now for the perfect venue. Lily should start by asking around, getting some good referrals. For what she had in mind, a chain place wouldn't cut it.

He was going to love it! Her feet did a little patter dance under her desk.

Brandon had been working so hard lately. The stress had begun to take its toll on their relationship. She wasn't exactly complaining, alright maybe she was, but she'd known going into this relationship that he was a serious CEO, committed and driven. If he wasn't working, he was thinking about work, well, except for those times when he wasn't. But even their intimate time together was getting more infrequent.

Her focus returned to her computer screen as a work email came through. She could figure out the details later. Work demanded her attention, and she was all too happy to comply.

Brandon studied his calendar for the last two weeks of the year. Meetings and more meetings with every major division of the company. Sales were strong, as usual, but the bottom line might not be what Wall Street expected since the Corticelli purchase would hit the books.

Brandon ran a hand through his hair. He'd had to cancel dinner with Lily the prior night, and he had been late for dinner at her place before that.

Donna buzzed his speakerphone. "Ten minutes until your meeting with Ken. Can I get you a cup of coffee?"

"Thanks, Donna. That'd be great."

Times like this Brandon felt overwhelmed. He didn't want to admit it out loud, but it was a fact. He spun in his office chair to stare out the twenty-story window to downtown Dallas. As much as he believed in Laurel and all the wonderful work they did, sometimes he wondered what life would be like with less responsibility. He'd felt the sting of resentment toward his father's illness that left him and his sisters in charge. Saying it out loud sounded cruel, so he would never complain. And on many levels, he was blessed. But for once he had something outside of work that meant the world to him and he struggled to fit it all in.

What would life be like with simpler things? Would he enjoy a small house with a picket fence and a dog? Could he live within a budget instead of buying anything he wished without thinking about the price tag? If he were a simpler man would he have even *met* Lily?

Hopefully, after Laurel closed out the year, things would calm down. Then maybe he could take Lily on a trip, someplace with lots of sun and sand. Lily in a bikini, lying next to him on the beach, would be the best vacation he could ask for.

***

From her office on Thursday Lily called up to Donna's desk. She hadn't had much interaction with the woman since Donna learned about her and Brandon seeing each other. Not that Lily would have much need to talk with her. She and Brandon had agreed to keep their relationship on the down-low. And most communication from the transition team *officially* went through her boss, Tom Ashley.

114

Lily took in a deep breath, and clamped a hand over her bopping knee.

"Brandon Morgan's office. This is Donna."

"Donna, hello. This is Lily Bennett from the Corticelli Transition Team."

"Hi Lily. Great to hear from you. Are you calling for Mr. Morgan? He's at an off-site meeting."

She heard the hesitancy in the woman's voice. She probably wondered why, since Lily had Brandon's cell number, would she be going through Donna.

"I know. That's why I'm calling now. I, um, want to surprise Brandon, and I need your help."

"Ooh, sounds fun." She heard the lilt in Donna's voice.

She smiled with relief. "I want to get Brandon a professional massage. He's never had one. And he's been working so much lately, I think he'd really like it."

"I agree with you."

"Can you look at his schedule and tell me what evenings, like around six o'clock, he's available?"

"Sure, let me see." She heard Donna clicking on her keyboard. "Hmm, next week he's open Tuesday and Friday nights. And of course, the week after that is Christmas. Do you want those dates?"

"No, that's all right. I can make this work. I'll email you when I get the appointment booked. Okay?"

"Sure, sweetie. Sounds good, but don't wait too long. His schedule can get crazy fast."

"Don't I know it."

They said their goodbyes. Lily was really starting to like that woman. She was glad Brandon had someone like Donna on his staff.

Chapter 17

BRANDON ENTERED THE spa through the hotel lobby. Instantly, the inviting smell floating in the air and the soft music filled his senses. He inhaled. Vanilla mixed with something else, he thought.

The place was empty except for a woman at the reception desk..

"Good evening," she said with a smile. The brunette stood just a bit taller than Lily with high cheekbones and dark green eyes. Her skin was as flawless as her posture.

"Hi. I have an appointment at six o'clock for a massage."

"You must be Mr. Morgan. I'm Julieta." She glanced at the computer monitor one last time. "I've got you scheduled for a ninety-minute massage with Alva. She's one of our best. Right this way."

He followed Julieta to a private, dimly lit room. The walls were painted a warm amber color and an instrumental piece played over the speakers.

"Sir, Alva is from Sweden. She speaks very little English," Julieta stated. "Any trouble areas, muscle soreness, that need extra attention?"

"Um, my shoulders are tight."

To say he was out of his comfort zone was an understatement. Lily had been so excited— sparkling like he hadn't seen in a while—to give him his present. There was no way Brandon would take that away from her.

"Very well, sir. She will ask *ja* if the pressure is good. Feel free to tell her more or less."

He nodded. *This should be interesting.*

"Please undress and get comfortable under the blanket, face up. Place this towel over your eyes, as the darkness will help with the relaxation." Julieta spoke softly and with authority, her hands clasped in front of her. "Any questions?"

"No. I appreciate it."

"Very well. Enjoy." Julieta turned about and gently closed the door behind her.

Brandon glanced around. Several hooks held hangers. He lifted one and slipped his suit jacket over a wooden hanger. He sat on the bench and left his cell phone, checking that it was off, on the side table. He removed his shoes and socks. Then, stood to remove everything else.

Admittedly, this experience felt foreign. The confidence that Alva was a trained professional propelled him forward. He had no reason to be nervous or bashful. He knew enough to know, he would be covered where it mattered. He might even fall asleep.

Getting between the covers, he placed the small, soft towel over his eyes. The relaxation began to settle in.

A brief moment later, he heard the door open.

"'ello." The clipped female voice led him to believe it was Alva.

"Hello." It felt strange not to make eye contact, but then again, he wasn't there for a business meeting.

He felt warm soft hands smooth over his pecs, then he heard what sounded like the lid of the lotion bottle and hands rubbing together.

Alva folded the sheet down to mid-chest, and laid her hands across and up his chest, working in strong, circular motions.

She positioned herself at the head of the table and worked his neck and shoulders. She had soft hands, but perhaps she could apply some more pressure.

"*Ja?*"

"It's nice. Maybe more pressure, Alva."

"*Ja.*"

She added some more pressure, and Brandon relaxed further. An occasional image of Lily appeared in his mind, and he tamped down a smile. She was a sweetheart to give him this gift, to think of him. That would be the ultimate present, though, a massage by Lily. Images of Lily, scantily clad, massaging his body—his *entire* body—filled his mind.

His dick flexed, and he quickly shifted and forced his thoughts to something benign.

"*Ja?*" Alva asked.

"I'm fine."

Brandon had been distracted and hadn't realized Alva had moved to massaging his arms. The movements were really quite good, he especially

118

liked the hand and wrist massage. Firm, but gentle. And something else. Sensual? Yes, perhaps that's a good word to describe it. But he demanded his mind not think in those terms or he'd have to contend with an embarrassing erection. Not that Alva turned him on. Hell, he hadn't even laid eyes on the woman. Maybe it was the *idea* that he could share this with Lily.

Adding more lotion to her hands, she uncovered his right leg and began the massage, using long firm strokes. It was nice, but it could be firmer. Time spent training at the gym often left his muscles sore, too much lactic acid. More pressure could help, but he didn't bother to say anything. If she asked, maybe.

Alva's hands on that last pass went a little higher then he'd expected. His breath hitched.

"*Ja?*"

"I'm fine." He felt like a parrot repeating himself.

She'd moved on, and he decided not to give it much more thought. Then she slid the covering off his left leg. Both legs were mostly uncovered. *Maybe that's a European thing.*

Her hands moved in long, firm strokes. He would relax more if the experience didn't feel so arousing. He willed his dick to stay down as Alva's hands climbed higher up his thigh before returning to his calf.

With both hands, Alva squeezed and stroked his thigh, fingers encircling most of it, working it up and down. Then she added more lotion and repeated the process on his right thigh, moving damn-near centimeters from his nuts. His breath caught.

Maybe it was a good time to tell Alva he wanted to flip over.

Oh fuck! One hand on each thigh, she slid up under the cover, over his hip joint, connecting around his semi-erect cock.

His heart jumped in his chest. He grabbed the towel off his face and flung it. "Alva!"

His head lifted and he focused on the woman giving him the soon-to-be erotic massage. Only, it looked like . . .

"Lily?"

"Yes, my love."

"Oh, sweet Jesus. Come here."

She smiled, removed her hands, and went to him. He pulled her down for a deep kiss, thrashing his tongue against hers.

He broke the kiss and panted. "I almost jumped off the fucking table." He could now state that with a grin on his face.

"Let me finish what I started. This is your present."

He looked at her more closely—she'd dressed casually.

Lily stood tall, and clasping the hem of her t-shirt, she pulled it over head, revealing a nude, see-through bra. Then she went to work on her jeans, sliding them to the floor and stepping out. She wore matching see-through panties.

"Fuck, you look hot." His dick was more than ready to play.

"Relax, if you can," she whispered with a grin.

She gave him a quick kiss on the lips, then from his abdomen, her lips headed south. Pushing the blanket down, her mouth easily covered his dick, causing him to groan. His hand instinctively went to her head and wove his fingers through her hair.

She fisted him and covered him as completely as she could.

Fuck!

She sucked on the way up, and Brandon's hips convulsed. His hand caressed her back and her bare luscious ass.

She licked and sucked, the slurping sound as loud as the music. He didn't have long to go. His woman gave him the best fucking head of his life.

"Ah," he called out and let his seed spurt into her mouth. She drank him, sucking him dry, and licking him clean.

Gee-zus!

She covered his parts and leaned close to his face. He opened his eyes to her sparkling smile. "Brandon, I love you. Merry Christmas. If you aren't mad at me—"

He grabbed the nape of her neck. "I'm not mad at you. I could never be mad at you. This was wonderful."

He started to raise his torso, and she pushed him down. "If you're not mad at me, you have a *real* massage coming. Her name is Ming. If you feel more comfortable, you can roll over, and she'll just work your back side."

Shit! Could he do this? Maybe now that Lily had drained him, he could. The pleading look in Lily's eyes told him he should at least try.

"Okay."

"Perfect."

He rolled over, and after Lily dressed she went to the door, and called out. In less than a minute, a short, smiling Asian woman with graying hair at the temples appeared. "Ming, this is Brandon. He likes medium to firm pressure. He's all yours."

She replied with a smile and a small bow.

Then Lily kissed Brandon and whispered. "I'll see you at home."

He grinned. That was the first time she'd referred to his place as home, and he loved it.

"Okay," he said with a wink. "Thank you."

Ming properly arranged his covers, revealing his back, and then she worked some lotion into her hands. She made a few wide passes then started to work his shoulder muscles specifically.

Wow! She dug her fingers in, working out knots, dragging across long muscles, and back again. Lily's touch was good, but more slide and glide. Ming was a little dynamo. Her experience was evident. She hunted out his trouble spots, and eased the tension and soreness in his muscles.

Well, hell! He couldn't believe he'd waited this long to have a professional massage. Now he knew why people were so addicted to these things.

It was beyond amazing, and Lily needed to know it.

This was wonderful.

Brandon's words played over and over in her mind. Best use of her bonus money! Well, not that she'd used it all. Hardly. Laurel was extremely generous with end-of-year bonuses and she felt blessed especially because she'd only started working there four months ago.

She practically danced around the condo, giddy with glee.

Her primary focus, though, was getting some relaxation for Brandon. He spent so much time at the office lately that she hardly saw him.

The manager at the spa had been so accommodating. She asked specific questions about how Lily wanted everything to play out. Lily blushed when she mentioned she'd like time alone first, then the official massage could begin.

The understanding smile on the woman's face had told her she knew Lily's exact motivation for wanting to give this special treat to Brandon.

Lily strode to the kitchen to see what the cook had left them for dinner that she could start.

She exhaled. Sometimes, guilt overwhelmed her. A nice girlfriend wouldn't be greedy with the time of her busy successful boyfriend, right? She didn't like this needy side of herself very much.

How ironic. They worked at the same company, but they could go days without seeing each other. Mostly, they had the weekends, but even at that, Brandon would get a call or need to do work on his computer.

She heard Brandon's voice before she heard the door and spun around as Brandon walked in. His case and jacket in his hand, his tie loosened, and his cell phone to his ear.

"Hang on a second, Marcus."

He went straight to Lily and placed a kiss on her lips. He smiled before he said, "I need to finish this. Go ahead and get started. I'll be out in a bit. And thank you again."

"Oh, okay."

A bit? Not likely, she thought.

She'd actually hoped he'd come in, wound up from his massage, and take her on the kitchen table. Or maybe from behind, standing against the cabinets, like he'd done at the dance club. Or even just pour them each a glass of wine and sit while they talked over dinner. She sighed as he disappeared from sight.

She didn't care what or where, she wanted to be with him.

Chapter 18

THE WEEK AFTER Christmas had been a crazy one, leaving Brandon more tense than usual.

Christmas day had been indescribable. No interruptions—zero—and it was absolute heaven. They'd slept in. She'd awoken to Brandon's large warm hands caressing and massaging her naked body. He brought her to a frenzy slowly, building the heat inside, and never letting it release. He savored her body like she was a seven-course meal. By the time she climaxed, she came so long and hard, she thought she'd pass out from the intensity. After breakfast, she went down on her knees to return the delicious favor. They'd lounged in their pajamas, watching Christmas movies, laughing, and eating. At some point—maybe after the pillow fight—they showered together, and Brandon held her up against the tile wall, making love to her until she screamed out his name. Dinner was scrumptious, and they managed to talk about things other than Laurel.

It was simply the most incredible day they'd ever had together.

January came in like a typhoon and stole their precious time, shoving in its place the demands of the presidency of a major, multinational corporation.

Some days, Lily just wanted to cry. She felt lonely and missed being with Brandon. Sometimes, even when he was present, he wasn't.

She'd decorated her apartment, organized her closet and kitchen pantry, worked out like a fiend when she wasn't in Rome, and learned how to play games with Court on her phone. Mostly stupid stuff to fill her hours when she wasn't working.

Courtney was so supportive. Lily didn't know what she would do without her best friend.

Naturally, she'd been spending more time at her own place since Brandon worked so late. At one point she'd asked him about his working hours. To his credit, he tried his damnedest not to get defensive.

I know. I don't like the crazy hours any more than you do. It won't last long. I promise.

She didn't feel very convinced, because no sooner had he said the words when his phone chimed with a text. She could swear he was trained by the ding on his phone.

They were on their way to Katie and Tim's for dinner; Brandon had put his sister off long enough. Katie had been trying to have them over for dinner since *before* she got married.

Staring out the car window, Lily sighed absently.

"Everything alright?" Brandon asked.

She glanced his way. "Yes. I'm good," she replied, not wanting to ruin the evening by bringing up the fact that it frightened her how little they got to see each other anymore.

"I guess it's good that we're finally making this happen. It's supposed to snow next week."

"Oh, wow. I didn't know that. I should probably have the tires on my car checked out."

Just great. Their conversation was now reduced to talking about the weather.

They drove almost forty minutes in silence. Brandon had so much on his mind, it was distracting. He took in a breath as he pulled into the circle drive of Katie's two-story contemporary home.

He grabbed the bottle of wine, and jogged around to Lily's side to open her door. She lifted the dessert off her lap and swung her high-heeled boots out of his sports car. She looked like a million bucks with the black leather jacket he bought her, her soft sweater, wool skirt, and tall black boots.

He offered his arm and led her to the door.

"Hey guys! You made it! Come in. Come in." Katie greeted them with exuberant hugs and kisses.

Tim walked into the foyer. "Hey guys. Welcome. Let me take your coats."

"Thank you," Lily said with a smile.

"Can I get y'all a drink?" Katie asked as she waved them to follow her into the kitchen.

"Sounds good," Brandon replied.

The kitchen was built for a chef with a six-burner cooktop, double ovens, hot water pot filler, and a huge stainless steel sink. The cabinets were a soft gray and the countertops looked like marble. Brandon heard a few of the details as Katie and Tim were going through the remodel; it was great to see the final product.

"Katie, your home is beautiful," Lily said his exact thoughts.

The four converged around the large island in her kitchen while Tim opened a bottle of white wine.

"Thank you. We like it. It's a bit of a drive to work, but totally worth it." Then she went to the stove to stir something.

"Anything I can do to help?" Lily asked.

"No, sit for a bit. Enjoy your wine. We're having shrimp scampi, but maybe we can have our salads first." Katie looked at Brandon in question.

"Sure," he replied.

"So," Tim opened the conversation, "Katie tells me Laurel announces earnings next week."

Shit! Lily hated too much shop talk when they were on their own personal time.

"Well, it should be interesting to say the least." He had an uneasy feeling in his gut about it truly, but he really didn't want to get into it.

"But we don't need to talk shop. How was your honeymoon? Tell us all about it." Lily's smile didn't touch her eyes.

Katie beamed at her new husband. "Well, it was simply the best," she began.

And the conversation steered to something other than work, which was a relief. He grabbed Lily's hand under the table and gave it a gentle squeeze. Her lips curved slightly.

Over dinner, the conversation continued, but not always as effortlessly. Thankfully his sister had a motor-mouth, and always had a topic ready if things got too stale.

After dinner, Katie stood. "I have delicious tiramisu from a local bakery. Bran, why don't you give me a hand?"

"Sure." He rose and took some empty plates with him.

"I hear you have to go to Rome a lot. I've never been. What's it like?" Brandon heard Tim ask Lily as he walked into the kitchen.

He lightly rinsed the dishes and stacked them in the dishwasher as Katie got dessert ready.

"So I noticed things seem strained between you and Lily." His sister pulled no punches.

He didn't bother to look at her. "Really?"

She stepped closer, likely not wanting to be overheard. "Don't play coy with me, brother. I know you too well."

He closed the dishwasher, and sighed. "They are, but you know how the end of year can be."

"It's a new year now, Bran."

"Well, we haven't announced earnings yet." He swung his hand aimlessly in the air. "After that, things will settle down."

"And then there will be quarterly earnings, and products launches, and—"

"Okay. Okay. I get your point." Why did he feel so hopeless some days?

She rested a hand on his upper arm, her soft eyes penetrating him. "Pull back, delegate more, and you don't have to be in the know or on top of everything. Laurel won't be any less successful by you doing those things."

He shrugged.

"At least think about. I can see that it's taking a toll on your relationship with Lily. You don't want to lose her, Bran."

His eyes widened. "No I don't, and I won't," he told her with conviction.

Hell no was he going to lose Lily. He'd spent months without her, let her walk out his life, and he'd sworn to himself if she ever came back, that wouldn't happen again.

The evening ended on a positive note, and Brandon couldn't wait to get Lily home where he could prove his love for her.

He reached across the center console of his car, and took her hand. "Would you please spend the night at my house?"

Before she could answer, his phone rang through his Bluetooth.

Dammit! Hadn't he turned the obtrusive thing off?

He saw the caller name on the screen and sent it to voicemail.

Glancing her way, he saw that her lips were pulled between her teeth. "Just you and me. The phone will be off."

She stared at him for a moment, and finally answered. "Okay."

Exactly what he wanted to hear.

They arrived back at his place, and he immediately turned off his phone. They were tired, but he didn't let that stop them. He took off her clothes and his, and made love to her in his bed. It wasn't the most spectacular sex they'd ever had, but it felt incredible to connect with Lily. He told her several times he loved her and he meant it, even if he had trouble showing it.

Soon, he told himself, things would get back to normal.

Chapter 19

LILY'S MOOD LIFTED a little. She'd survived the week not seeing Brandon, and it was Friday. Better still, Brandon was home. Although he was still in his office. She peeked one more time into the oven.

The chicken is drying out.

She went to Brandon's office and rapped lightly before entering.

"Lily," he yelled. "I need a few more minutes. Start without me." Intensity burned from his dark eyes.

He glanced back at his computer screen, not another word or glance toward her. No apology.

He'd never yelled at her before. He had been tense these last few weeks, she could feel it roll off him when he'd come home. But it had never been like this. She lost her appetite.

She backed away and quietly closed his office door.

Tears pricked the backs of her eyes and she knew she'd better hide her face fast. The embarrassment of Brandon seeing her like this would be more than she could bear. She ran to the bathroom, and grabbed a towel to stifle her sobs.

Oh God. Now she'd seen Brandon mad. She shouldn't take it personally. He was under a lot of stress. He made an effort to be there for dinner, but within five minutes of walking through the door, he was in his office.

She'd been looking forward to a quiet night, just the two of them, dinner and a movie while cuddling on the sofa.

Another sob escaped.

She couldn't compete with his company, with the insane amount of responsibility hanging over his head. She couldn't compete.

She replayed a conversation they'd had in Rome when he'd told her, *Work will always come first for me.*

She wiped more tears that streamed down her cheeks. *I can't win. I will always be second to Laurel.*

Lily cried for several more minutes before gathering herself together and getting ready for bed. She didn't know what she was going to do, but she'd cried herself to exhaustion so she'd have to think of something later.

At almost midnight, Brandon switched off the lights to his office. What a cluster-fuck!

He rubbed the heels of his hands in his eye sockets. Wall Street was pissed that earnings were lower than expected. *Seriously?!* He'd bought a company for the love of God! The board was acting flustered about it. *They've had decades of pure bliss, and one bump, they all freak.* And if he received one more inquiry letter from the FDA, he would likely scream.

He popped the top off a beer bottle and chugged half of it down.

The icing on the cake? He'd yelled at Lily. He shook his head. What the fuck was he thinking?

He polished off his beer, and made his way to the bedroom where, just as he suspected, he found Lily curled up at the edge of the bed asleep.

He brushed his teeth and replayed the events of the last few days. Work had been busy before, sometimes a little crazy, but this took the fucking cake. He wanted to shield most of the b.s. from Katie and Leena, but how much longer could he keep them in the dark? And he was taking it out on Lily.

He stripped down to his boxer briefs and climbed between the sheets. He pulled her closer into him, and heard her sob. His breath hitched. He switched on the side table lamp. Her eyes were closed, still asleep. She sobbed in her sleep and didn't even know it.

His heart constricted, and he rubbed a hand over his face. He'd done this. And if he didn't fix it soon, his relationship with Lily would be at risk. If it wasn't already.

***

Lily awoke with an ache in her heart. All the emotion from the previous night came rushing back, feeling just as fresh.

She turned toward the empty place in the bed beside her. Brandon was gone. It was barely seven and the condo was desolately quiet.

She dragged herself from bed, and after a stop in the bathroom, headed to the kitchen for coffee. Caffeine would possibly get her through the day. She flopped down onto a chair at the table and stared into nothing.

What was she going to do? She and Brandon were becoming more and more distant. She struggled between giving him space to run his company and wanting time alone with him.

Was it too early to call Court?

She glanced at her phone. Yes.

She plodded to the shower and blasted the water. The bathroom held a faint smell of Brandon's cologne. He wore the best cologne. She would always associate that mix of sandalwood and citrus with him.

Her eyes clouded, so she quickly stripped out of her boxers and t-shirt, and stepped under the spray. She let a few tears stream down her face as she scrubbed her body. She would get all of this out now, before she went to the office. Crying at the office did not evoke confidence from her team.

Brandon was on yet another call with investors. Since Laurel had announced earnings, that's all he fucking did. Institutional investors, mutual funds, CBNC, everyone and their brother wanted to fucking talk about how he was going to turn the company around.

What. The. Fuck.

He'd purchased a company and moved corporate headquarters. One-time expenses. It happened all the time in Corporate America. So one time, there would be an outlay of cash—cash they had—and that would be it. All future earnings reports would be just as expected.

"Sales were still up for the quarter *and* for the year, Brian," he spoke to the man on the phone, who worried over whether he should dump his holdings in Laurel or not.

Laurel's stock was down almost twenty percent. Who knew what kind of a hit his personal portfolio had taken.

Every investor, if they were smart, would look at it as if the stock was on sale. Jim Cramer could say that, not him.

Brian rambled on some more. Brandon justified and walked through the numbers, once again.

For the first time, he regretted buying Corticelli. The whole acquisition created a mound of headache that simply wasn't worth it.

When the acquisition was announced, Wall Street practically came in their drawers. They couldn't have been happier. And now that it was done . . .

Did they think the company had been free?

The best thing from the Corticelli deal was Lily. If not for the deal, he wouldn't have met her. He'd found a love that reached him deep inside. A woman that made him want more out of life. A woman who made him lower his guard, and think about something other than Laurel—something that revolved around a wife and children.

Now, if he could get a moment of peace to share with her—like they'd had in the beginning.

He shook his head at the entire mess. Brian finally got off the phone, and he had a minute to breathe. It was only two o'clock and he wanted a drink.

He wanted to call Lily, but he had no time. He shot her a quick text.

I'm sorry I missed you this morning. Phone glued to my ear today. I hope you are having a good day. See you tonight?

She replied a minute later.

OK. I'll come to your place.

He let out a sigh of relief. He'd actually wondered if she'd respond. Her text was short, but he shouldn't expect anything different, really. Jewelry wouldn't get him out of this mess.

Lily saw Brandon's text and wanted to cry. He had left that morning without a goodbye. That was the third time he'd done that. All of it, that month.

She sighed and stared up at the ceiling. Now would be a good time to call Court. She'd be on her lunchbreak.

Can you talk?

Courtney's reply text came right back.

Yes.

She walked away from her cube, down the hall to an empty conference room.

"Hey babe. What's up? How's the Big D?" Her vivacious voice bubbled over the phone.

"Hey, Court. Not so good."

"What's wrong?"

"I haven't talked about it much, but Brandon is working more. Longer hours."

She gasped. "You don't think he's having an affair, do you?"

Lily smiled. Her first real smile in a while. "No. He's too devoted to his company, but Court, I miss him. I miss *us*."

"Oh, babe. Have you talked to him? What does he say?"

"Very little. He said he doesn't like it either, but there's nothing he can do. I don't know Court. Sometimes, I think he takes on more than he needs to. Like, how is it that most of the company's executives can play golf and take vacation time?"

"Hmm, maybe they aren't as devoted. And it's really *his* company."

"I know that, and that's what it comes down to." Her voice dropped an octave. "I can't compete with Laurel. I'm seriously wondering if I made a mistake coming out here."

"Oh, babe. What are you gonna do?"

"I don't know."

After a brief pause, Courtney said, "Why don't you come out here? Stay with me for a couple of days. Get some space to think about your next move."

Lily wiped a few stray tears that had fallen. That actually sounded like a good idea. She wasn't expected in Rome for another month. "I can look into it."

"Good. I'll have to work, but my boss will give me a few half days. At least you can get some peace. We can hang out in our pajamas, eat pizza and chocolate, and watch The Wedding Date a million times."

She chuckled. "Okay, I'll text you."

They said their goodbyes, and she dashed into the ladies room to check her makeup. Now, the big thing, how to tell her boss she needed to leave suddenly. She didn't know how that would be received. She hated the idea of leaving the company in a lurch like this, but she needed her best friend. The desperation from the last few weeks and months . . . well, she just couldn't be around here for a while.

After combing the airline sites, she found a pretty reasonably priced ticket to LA. Departure was early in the morning, and it was just two days away. Holy crap!

Better get it approved before I make the purchase.

She strode to Tom's office and rapped lightly on the door jamb.

He glanced up from his computer screen. "Lily. Come in. What can I do ya' for?"

"Hey, Tom. Something's come up. A personal matter that I need to take care of. I need to go back to California for a few days, maybe a week."

He furrowed his brows. "Sure, absolutely. Anything I can do?"

"No, thank you. I'm sure it will smooth out soon." *At least that's the lie I tell myself.*

"Okay. When do you need to leave?"

"The day after tomorrow."

All credit to Tom, if he was surprised he didn't show it in the least. He simply nodded. "Okay. Please let the team know."

"I will. Thanks so much, Tom."

"You're welcome. And good luck, Lily."

She slumped back into her seat, not feeling much better than when the day had started. The prospect of leaving for several days, being without Brandon, scared and relieved her at the same time.

What if she left, and he decided he didn't want to be with her anymore?

No! She couldn't think that.

Now she had to tell Brandon. Maybe he would appreciate the space too. Maybe she'd come back and things would be better. Maybe . . . maybe she'd come back and it would be exactly the same. The two of them not seeing each other for stretches at a time.

Shit! The fear and uncertainty was consuming her. She'd put her walls up before as it related to Brandon, and it was happening again. Going to LA would be good, to help her make a decision—which she couldn't do if he was in her orbit. She loved him, that was undeniable. But that also made her vulnerable.

Chapter 20

BRANDON'S STEPS FELT a little lighter on the pavement the closer he got to Lily. He owed her an apology from his behavior the previous night, and he was anxious to see her. He would need to find a way to make it up to her. He just couldn't think of anything right then—he was mentally exhausted.

He walked into his condo and found Lily looking out his picture window. She turned when she heard the door. She wore her work clothes. Her arms were crossed, and her face read wary.

"Hi."

"Hi."

He slung his jacket over the back of the chair, dropped his case, and walked to her. He took her hands in his, staring down at them for beat.

"I owe you an apology for last night. I was on edge. So much is going on right now, and I'm not thinking clearly when it comes to my personal life."

"Yes, I see that," she said softly.

He leaned into her and kissed her forehead.

"Can you forgive me?" he said against her soft skin.

"Yes."

Thank God. He felt as if a weight had been lifted. "I'm lucky to have you, Lily." He gave her another peck, resisting more when really he just wanted to devour her. He'd missed being with her, feeling her naked warm body lying next to him at night, sated from hours of love making.

Maybe tonight . . .

He pulled back, letting his lips curve as he looked into her gorgeous blue eyes. Dinner, then love making. Surely he could find the energy for that.

"Are you hungry?" He released her hands and headed for the kitchen in hopes of something delicious to strengthen him.

She cleared her throat. "Um, Brandon." He turned around expecting her to make some quip about make-up sex first. Instead her eyes shown somber, maybe even sad.

"I am going to California to stay with Courtney for a while. I've cleared it with Tom."

A desolate feeling washed over Brandon. He stepped back. "California?"

"Yes." Her eyes welled. "I'm not exactly sure for how long, but I need to get away. Take a break. I've been feeling . . . overwhelmed lately. So much has happened these last few months, and well, I need some time to myself."

He was speechless. What he feared most was playing out before him, and he was powerless to stop it. "Are you leaving me?"

Tears streamed down her cheeks. She shook her head.

He made a step closer. "Is that a no?"

"No. I don't know. I don't want to but I don't know what to do. That's why I'm taking a break for a little while."

He wanted to howl. The one woman he loved, truly loved, outside of family, was thinking about leaving him.

"I wish you wouldn't. Did you quit Laurel?"

She shook her head. "No. I love my job."

That's something.

"When are you leaving?"

She glanced down. "Day after tomorrow."

Fuck!

"Okay. Can I call you and text you?"

The corner of her lips lifted infinitesimally. "Yes."

"Is there anything I can say to make you stay?"

"No. I'm sorry."

He reached for her hands and she let him. "Don't be sorry. I know why you need to go, well, not really, but I respect it."

She smiled as more tears ran down her cheeks. She pushed up on her toes and swung her arms around him. He pulled her close, not wanting to let her go. He held her for as long as she let him.

"Will you stay for dinner?"

She broke their bond. "No, I can't. I need to go." And in the same breath, she reached down for her purse and headed for the door. "Goodbye, Brandon."

The door opened, and Lily walked out.

He stood stock-still for several moments, staring at the door. He wanted to run after her, but he knew she needed her space.

He scrubbed a hand over his face and plodded to the kitchen to retrieve his bottle of whiskey, gripping it like he was ready to heave it.

Sure, he would give her some space. For a little while. But frankly, he didn't think his heart could handle much more. He'd lost her once—perhaps he hadn't fought hard enough for her—but he would not make that same mistake twice. He may be thick sometimes, but he wasn't stupid.

With three fingers worth of whiskey in his glass, he went to his balcony and slumped down on a chair. It was too damn cold to be outside, but a few minutes wouldn't kill him. He needed to feel something other than the gash in his heart.

Today, he would lick his wounds and feel like complete shit. Tomorrow, he'd get to work. Not company work, but getting-Lily-back work. This was all his fault and he needed to fix it. And he suspected he didn't have much time.

***

Brandon awoke with one thought on his brain. Lily. This could be the best year of his life or the worst.

His plan was to make it the former.

He strode off the elevator toward his office with purpose. His head may have felt heavy as shit, but he had too much to do to let that stop him.

Passing Donna's desk, he called. "Donna, would you kindly bring me a *strong* cup of coffee?"

"Yes, of course."

"Thank you."

After booting up his computer, he opened the file he wanted to see—a list of every single product Laurel made. *Gees!*

Donna strolled in, and the smell of coffee filled the room. She set the cup on his desk and looked at him, and after a pause, said, "I heard."

"So that means—"

She raised a hand. "Nobody knows about you two. I put it together."

"I'm not surprised," he said with a remorseful smile.

"What are you going to do?"

He clicked through the side of his mouth. "Haven't quite got that worked out yet."

"Okay, let me know if I can help."

She spun around to leave but before she made it to the door, he called out, "Donna."

Donna turned to face him.

With his cup raised, he said, "Keep it comin'."

She smiled before replying, "Yes, your majesty."

First calls were to his sisters. He would need their input and approval if he was to come up with a solution that involved Laurel.

"Hey, Katie. I want to have a meeting—you, me, and Leena. Any chance you can clear your calendar one day this week?"

"The whole day?" she replied as her voice rose.

"Yes."

"Sounds serious."

"It is." *Damn serious.*

"Okay."

"Get back to me as soon as you can. Also, can you field any calls from investors?"

"Sure."

He hung up the phone and began planning. He made a list of folks he would need to talk to, financial documents they'd want to review, and of course, which products—

Donna broke his stream of thought. "Brandon, sorry to bug you. Marcus is on the phone for you. And at nine Roberta was going to give you an update from R and D."

"Great. Thanks for the reminder. Put Marcus through."

He lifted the phone to his ear. "Marcus, I was just thinking about you."

"Oh boy, that can't be good."

He chuckled. Brandon truly worked with some of the best people. "I got something I want to discuss, on the down-low. Do ya have any time in your schedule this afternoon or tomorrow?"

He gave Marcus an overview of what he was thinking without getting into the personal motivation behind it. And Marcus didn't ask. The man agreed to gather some of the financials Brandon needed and meet him at two that afternoon. *Perfect.*

He buzzed Donna. "Would you send all investor calls to Katie? And I doubt I need to ask, but I'm going to need some clear blocks of time in my schedule this week, and one full day with Katie and Leena."

"Already working on it. An updated calendar should be on your PC in a few minutes."

"You are a godsend."

"Yes, I am." And she disconnected the line.

He chuckled at her easy humor. Cell phone in hand, Leena would be his next call.

"Bran. How's life in the Big-D?"

"Hey, Leena. I'm fine, but could be better. Let's talk business."

"Okay. Shoot."

He filled her in on his idea and asked if she could fly out to meet with him and Katie.

"Bran, I love it. This is probably long overdue."

How right she was.

"Thanks. I'll see you soon."

He tossed his phone to the desk and exhaled. For the first time in a while, Brandon thought maybe, just maybe, there was a light at the end of the tunnel. And it wasn't an oncoming train!

***

In the days that followed, Brandon focused on work and what he had to do to save his relationship with Lily. He went to the gym to work up a sweat and mitigate at least some of the stress pressing down on him. He slept in four hour stretches, at most. He didn't have much of an appetite, but he ate anyway. His heart ached for Lily.

He'd had a taste of what life could be like with a woman, a woman he loved. Up until meeting Lily, he'd successfully avoided love relationships, just because of his work demands. Rachel was proof of his success rate.

Lily was different. There was something about her. He smiled as he stared out the window. She was kind and smart. She was self-assured, and yet vastly underestimated the effect she could have on men.

By the end of the week, he had most of his plan in motion. Katie and Leena were behind him one-hundred percent. He had Donna making his travel plans.

Engrossed in an email from an interested party, his cell phone rang. He was only mildly surprised that it was from his father.

"Hey, Dad."

"Son, I understand you've a lot going on over there in Dallas."

Well, shit, here it comes. "Yes, I do." He braced himself for a downpour. But he'd rehearsed what he'd tell his father. He was prepared.

"I see." His father lowered his voice as he proceeded. "I'm glad you're doing this."

Now that caused Brandon's jaw to drop. "Glad?"

His dad's tone soft with sincerity. "Yes, of course. This is really something I should have done when I had the helm. Might have saved a lot of headaches." His voice tinged with melancholy.

Wow! He hadn't expected that kind of support from his father. His mother, yes, but not his father. He'd built this company from the ground up. He had a will of iron. How many times had Brandon heard his father say *Kids, never rest on your laurels. You either excel, or be excelled.* Hence, the name of the company.

Yet, the whole family knew, in many ways, that had almost cost him his life.

"Dad, thanks for the support. Did my sisters also tell you why I'm doing this?"

"They mentioned there was a girl."

"That's right."

"Is it Lily, from Katie's wedding?"

"Yes."

"I really like her. Go get her, boy." His chuckle rang in Brandon's ear.

Damn straight!

Chapter 21

SHE SAT ON Courtney's sofa, sipping a hot tea. Day six without Brandon. And she felt no closer to any sort of decision. That wasn't entirely true, she had made one decision. She was going to fight for her man. She just didn't know how. She may come to regret not cutting ties. But she knew one thing for sure, she would regret it if she didn't try.

There had to be a way where she could create boundaries, though, and not become a doormat. She wanted her job, and she wanted him; she had to find a way to make it work.

Maybe he can commit to Sundays?

At the very least she'd have to reset her expectations. The vital question was, would this be enough to sustain them? Was this enough of a foundation to build a life on?

Over the last six days, they'd traded texts and spoken a few times. She could tell he had something important on his mind. His voice was clear and his speech fast, almost determined. At one point, he told her *we will figure this out, Lily.* She'd sobbed for several minutes after that call. She just wasn't sure *how* they could make it work.

By three that afternoon, she found it odd that he hadn't at least texted her that day. Maybe he'd figured it out and knew they should just call it quits, but wanted to wait to tell her in person.

Tears threatened to rain down. She *couldn't* let herself believe that.

But if they broke up, what of her job? She didn't lie when she told Brandon she loved her job. If she stayed, how exactly would that work? The fear of running into him would have her heart breaking all over again. She might not be strong enough to withstand that kind of pain.

She reached for her phone to see when yoga class started. She needed a distraction. Before she could even get to the site, the doorbell rang. *Probably a delivery for Court.*

Lily peered through the peephole, and standing on the other side of the door was her heart's desire.

Seeing Brandon made her long for him while it broke her heart at the same time.

She opened the door. He wore a jacket, slacks, and a fine-knit sweater that fit him like a glove, showing off his strong torso. Slight dark shadows were evident under his eyes.

She wanted to leap into his arms and wrap herself around him. She stayed rooted. This could be good or this could be bad.

"Hi. What are you doing here?" she asked softly.

"I came to talk to you. May I come in?"

Foolish. "Of course." She stepped aside.

They walked a few feet into Courtney's living room, and she turned to face him. He scanned the place and shoved his hands in his pockets, wordless, as if he didn't know where to start.

"It took you leaving to make me realize what an ass I've been."

Her eyebrows lifted. She hadn't expected that.

His stare penetrated her. "You are special to me, Lily. I love you. I love everything about you. How patient you are with me, how understanding. And I've taken advantage of that." He reached for her hands. "I never told you this, but some days I dreaded going to work. I hated leaving you. Every day, day after day. You are the sunshine in my life. You are my life." He motioned with a tip of his head. "Can we sit?"

Her hands trembled and she didn't know why. He was here before her, fighting for her. Emotion raced through her in the most uncontrollable way. She wanted to hold him, she wanted to cry, she wanted to laugh . . .

"So, I'm making some changes. I already spoke to my family. There are pieces of the company we can divest—"

"What?! No. I'm not expecting you to choose," she pleaded, her head shaking back and forth.

He kissed the back of her hands. "Hear me out. There are product lines we don't need. We need to stay true to our core business. We've expanded over the past few years, and sure it was profitable, but not necessary for the long-term success of Laurel." He took in air, like he was trying to calm a racing heart. "I almost lost you once. I won't do it again. I'm miserable without you."

Tears welled in her eyes, and streamed down her cheeks. "I'm miserable without you too, Brandon. I miss you when you're not around. I thought my biggest competition was going to be other women, but it's Laurel."

He swiped away her tears with his thumbs. "I know, baby, and that's going to change."

He bent his knees and went down in front of her as he pulled a small black velvet box out of his jacket pocket. Her hands flew over her mouth. "Lily, I don't deserve you. You are warm and giving, with a heart the size of Texas. You came into my life and turned it upside down. I never envisioned life married, and now I can't imagine not being married to you. Please do me the honor of marrying me, being my wife. Together, for the rest of our lives."

An insanely beautiful two-carat diamond ring with baguettes on each side shone back at her. Sparkling brighter than anything she could imagine. He wanted to marry her. He was willing to sell off parts of the company to be with her. Forever.

On an exhale, she said, "Yes. I would *love* to marry you." The tears streamed down her cheeks again as he slipped the ring on her left hand.

He rose and grabbed her close, kissing her like his life depended on it. "I love you, Lily. You make me happy."

"I love you, too." She smiled through her tears of joy.

He wrapped his strong arms around her, tugging her so close, there was no space between them.

After a few moments, he asked, "Can we go somewhere?"

"Sure, but all my stuff is here."

"I know, we'll come back to get everything and say a proper goodbye."

She glanced around. "Okay." She slung her purse over her shoulder, and grabbed Brandon's outstretched hand.

In the limo, Brandon pulled her close, his arm resting on her shoulders, pressing small kisses against her hair. She reached for his other hand, laying it on her lap, basking in the glow of this surprising turn of events.

"Brandon, we need to talk about what we can do to avoid going down this hole in the future."

"I agree." He lifted her chin with his finger. "I'll be delegating more to Katie and Leena. And if it gets too much for all of us, we'll sell it. I can't have a family if I'm working all the time," he said with a wide smile across his lips.

"Family?"

"Absolutely." The sparkle in his eyes told her that would make him only too happy.

After a short drive, they arrived at a lovely old building downtown. She'd read about this hotel. It had been built decades ago by a large Italian family, and thrived ever since.

He led her through the hotel's lobby with several tall stone columns, and a fountain with greenery directly in the center. A feeling of being in Rome rushed through her.

Brandon pushed the elevator door button. "Feels like Italy, doesn't it?" he whispered in her ear.

He'd planned this. He was up to something. She grinned up at him.

He unlocked their suite door and guided her inside. She gasped. Candles. Candles everywhere. The drapes were drawn and not one light was on. Lily's gaze roamed over the several bouquets of flowers throughout the suite, and champagne chilling in an ice bucket.

He led her through the doorway into the bedroom.

Red rose petals were sprinkled all over the pristine-white, king-sized bed. "Brandon," she breathed.

He spun her around toward him. "I don't want to waste another moment starting the rest of our lives together. Text Courtney. Tell her you'll be by in the morning to get your things. This night, all night, you are mine. I will make love to you, feed you, hold you while you sleep, then we'll wake up and do it all again."

Her heart hammered against the wall of her ribcage.

"And the only thing you'll be wearing is my ring."

She glanced down at her left hand at her sparkling diamond ring. She was engaged.

Lily grabbed the phone from her purse, her thumbs flying as she sent a message to her best friend. She knew Courtney would understand. Then she set everything on the dresser top and faced him.

He smiled as he approached. Taking her jaw in his large warm hands, he kissed her deeply. His tongue claiming hers, willing her for more, giving her more.

His fingers grazed against her arms, up and down, sending tingles everywhere. His kiss traveled to her neck, gently sucking and licking.

He breathed against her ear. "My beautiful woman, strip for me."

Oh, yes. Feeling Brandon's hands and mouth all over her body, wanting to give pleasure more than receive, she'd happily comply.

He yanked an armless chair from the corner of the room and placed it where he could get his fill. She sighed watching him. His eyes darkened with passion, passion for her. *This man will be my husband.*

She realized it was no small coincidence that the bedroom had fewer candles lit compared to the main room. No doubt, Brandon had instructed someone to do that. Lily was getting more comfortable being naked in full-light with Brandon, and he was a patient man.

She started with her shoes, then her jeans slipped over her hips and to the floor. Next she yanked off her shirt overhead and dropped it.

"Freeze," he said.

He stood and proceeded to get naked for her, revealing his aroused hard body. *He's all mine.*

He returned to the chair. "Continue, please. Slowly."

She unhooked her bra, freeing her heavy breasts, and as slowly as she could, let the lacy confection fall to the floor.

He groaned. "Massage them for me, Lily."

She did as he requested, caressing and fondling, tugging at her nipples the way he'd taught her. He reached his right hand to his cock, stroking it. The head slowly turned a deep red.

"Panties now."

She hooked her thumbs through the waistband of her lace thong and slid it slowly to the floor to step out.

"Closer, please."

She moved closer and he leaned forward, to where his head was level with her stomach, closed his eyes and inhaled long and deep.

His large hands covered the crux of her buttocks at her upper thighs, and he laid several butterfly kisses on her tummy. "You smell like ambrosia. Are you wet, Lily?" he whispered to her body.

He glanced up as she nodded.

"Let me see, sweetheart." He gently guided her hand to her denuded sex, urging her on.

She reached her finger and slid it through her slickness. A mewl escaped.

"Legs wider. Do that again."

She did as he asked, then he held her hand and brought a wet finger to his mouth. It was so erotic to watch Brandon take her whole finger into his warm mouth and slowly pull it out clean.

"Hands on my shoulders."

He straightened in the chair and his legs closed. She made a half-step closer, straddling his thighs. A slow trickle of wetness slid down her inner thigh.

She stopped when his hands stroked her thighs and crept to her core, one hand over her mons, circling like a mini-massage. "I love to see all of you, Lily."

His other hand glided through her center and two wet fingers slid inside her.

"Mmm."

"It is so amazing to me how wet you get." He pumped several times. She let her head fall back, relishing his movements, every blessed touch.

"My fiancée, please come here."

With her hands on his shoulders and his hands supporting her waist, she shimmied closer and hovered over his erect cock. He held onto it with one

155

hand as she lowered herself down, inch by glorious inch. She could feel him go deeper inside her. She loved this position.

"Oh, God, Brandon."

He wrapped his arm around her, one hand cradling her neck. "Yes, my love." Then he brought her lips to his for a hungry, passionate kiss. She started to rock on him, and kissed him deeper.

Her muscles already started contracting around him.

"Brandon."

"Don't stop, baby."

He flexed his hips and dove deeper inside her which detonated her climax. She moaned loudly, let her head fall back, and rode him faster.

"Hold on." His words broke her spell. She wrapped her arms and legs around him, and he rose, carrying her to the high bed.

He gently set her on the mattress, but remained standing and inside her. He lifted her legs out wide, hands circled around her ankles. The way he stared down at her, her naked body, with his deep dark eyes, methodically pumping into her, was so erotic.

"I will never get enough of you, Lily."

She closed her eyes and moaned, over his words, over an impending climax.

"God, I missed you, Brandon."

As if not wanting to release too early, he stopped, let her legs down, and took in air.

He replaced his cock with two fingers and leaned over her. He placed several small kisses on her lips, her cheeks, and her neck.

"Lily."

"Yes, baby."

"I knew you were mine and we were meant to be together the day after you moved to Dallas. That's when I bought that ring."

Her eyes rounded, and she placed her left hand against his chest, his heart beat strong under her fingertips.

"That's when you told me you loved me."

He nodded.

"I love my ring. I love that you picked it out."

He smiled and pulled out his fingers to slide in his cock. "I may screw up again, Lily," he pumped slowly as he spoke, "but know that I am in love with you." He pressed her hand over his heart tighter. "You are my everything and I won't let you go."

He dove deeper into her, setting off both their releases at the same time.

"I love you, Brandon," she breathed in his ear, and he collapsed over her warm body.

"I love you, Lily. More than anyone could love another person."

And he sealed his lips to hers. The beginning of many kisses they had a lifetime to share.

Thank you for reading!

If you enjoyed this story, please consider posting a review at one or more of your favorite retailers. Even a short review, one or two lines, can be a tremendous encouragement to the author. Your review is also a gift to other readers who may be searching for just this sort of story and will be grateful that you helped them find it.

Thank you!

Other Books by Mia London

Life To The Max
Wanton Angel, Prequel to Life To The Max
Perfect Seduction (Perfect, 1)
Perfect Surrender (Perfect, 2)
Beyond Lace (Hard Men of the Rockies, 4)

ABOUT THE AUTHOR

Mia London loves to write.
After reading fiction for years, she decided it was finally time to put
those images and scenes floating around in her head down on paper.

She is a huge fan of romance, highly optimistic, and wildly faithful to
the HEA (happily ever after). Her goal is to create a fantasy you will
enjoy with characters you could love.

She lives in Texas with her attentive, loving, super-model husband, and
perfectly behaved, brilliant children. Her produce never wilts, there are
no weeds in her flowerbeds and chocolate is her favorite food group.

Facebook
Twitter
Goodreads
Webpage
Email: **mia@mialondon.com**

CPSIA information can be obtained
at www.ICGtesting.com
Printed in the USA
FFHW011015040519
52215686-57596FF